Tales of the Hidalgo Pump House

A two-act play
by Lucio G. Rivera
and Pedro Garcia

with a Special Edition
"Once Upon A Time Around Old Hidalgo"

Mission, Texas

ISBN-10: **0-9989965-4-8**
ISBN-13: **978-0-9989965-4-7**

To secure permission for presenting the play and information regarding the small royalty fee please contact Lucio G. Rivera at 956-905-4501 or Pedro Garcia at teatronuestra@hotmail.com or at 956-655-9308.

Table of Contents

Foreword

Ever wonder what a theater play looks like in its most raw form? Pedro Garcia and Lucio G. Rivera, two writers and veteran purveyors of art through theater, have teamed up to bring you "Tales of the Hidalgo Pump House". This book contains the play of the same title, along with a photo gallery of actors bringing the story to life on the stage. It features a short comic strip of supernatural beings and moments in the play illustrated and captioned by Mr. Rivera himself. This section is followed by a limited—yet interesting—historical account of the City of Hidalgo's settlement, as well as the people involved in different capacities in the development of the municipality and its pump house through multiple generations. The book closes with an ode to Hidalgo by Mr. Rivera.

  The reader will note that within the play itself the writers utilize both parentheses to distinguish the voice of directions given to actors by a director describing the setting or the characters' motivations during rehearsal. The parentheses also indicate a shift from director to narrator of the book speaking to a reader about what is happening on stage, like pauses and action. There is another voice that speaks to an audience or reader and is also called "Narrator". When the reader sees this, she or he will note that this voice is also one of the characters in the play who occasionally breaks the fourth wall and speaks directly to the live audience—within quotations—as well as to the reader. This format makes this book ideal for organizations and individuals who might not only seek to read a great story but, perhaps, even stage the play themselves.

  For more information on staging the play, please read the "Preface" by Pedro Garcia.

Preface
by Pedro Garcia

I have fond memories of my childhood growing up about two blocks from the old Hidalgo, Texas Pump House, or *la pompa*, as we all called it. I recall coming of age and swimming in the cool water basins during the hot summer days in the Rio Grande Valley in the 1970's. My uncle Lucio, who co-wrote this play with me, also recalls his teen days swimming in those delicious pools of water in the 1950's. We also enjoyed lots of fishing, such as catfish, gar, and carp. Our ancestors did the same, dating back to 1909 when the Pump House was inaugurated. Of course, we learned that the water was pumped from the Rio Grande, or the Rio Bravo (as the river is commonly known in Mexico) and used to irrigate nearby crops in the region. Our dinner tables always had the best vegetables and fruits to say the least.

The water was drawn up from the low-lying river by giant Hamilton Corliss and Ingersoll steam engines. These engines can be seen today at their original site at the pump house that is now a Museum and World Birding Center, in the City of Hidalgo. Everyone is welcomed to visit to learn the entire history. As a matter of fact, the whole pump house structure is still there with all its original machinery for all to see, thanks mainly to Dr. Robert Norton, who led the effort toward its preservation for its historical significance. Had it not been for Dr. Norton and other visionaries, who knows what would have happened to *la pompa*... when it pumped its last gallon of water in 1983. (Today modern electric engines operate the same function about half a mile down river from the old pump house).

In the beginning, local workers would feed mesquite wood from nearby clearings into boiler furnaces that created steam to operate the machines. It took many skilled pump house workers, like Rufus Wisdom, Luis Rivera, Pete Bosch, Luis Sweet and Eulalio Salas Huerta—to name a few—just to make sure the temperatures were perfect, and the engines were well oiled and calibrated. Later, when wood was no longer available, oil and then natural gas, were utilized.

When running on full force the old pump house could pump up to an amazing 408,000 gallons of water per minute (enough water to fill an Olympic-sized pool in 20 seconds) onto man-made basins, and flowing irrigation canals, and ditches to water crops in the surrounding fields. I also remember the constant clanking sounds of the huge pistons and machines, and how they created a heartbeat for our small community back then. We got used to the sound, and on rare occasions when the engines would stop for a day or two, the town became quiet and almost mysterious… (cue the ghostly laughter). That's when stories of the creepy characters that supposedly would appear around *la pompa* emerged from the older townsfolk; these were the stories they loved telling us of *La Llorona*/The Weeping Woman, *La Lechuza*/The White Owl Witch, *La Muerte*/Death and *El Hombre Sin Cabeza*/The Headless Man and La Mujer Vestida de Blanco. All of this energy made growing up in Hidalgo, Texas a blast for me and countless others.

It gives me great honor to present this play to you in written form, and I encourage all directors, historians, drama teachers, librarians, museum directors, and others to present a staging of this story for the communities and student bodies you represent. This play will not only entertain but will provide a rich history of the old Hidalgo Pump House and the people who knew it when it was alive!

Lastly, I wish to thank Lucio G. Rivera, my dad's youngest brother, for having approached me back in the early 2000's with a manuscript about his vision to tell this story via the stage. I also thank Dr. Elva and Dr. Keith Michal, founders and former colleagues of the Pharr Community Theater (PCT) for their help in the first production of the play back in 2011. Thanks, as well, to the cities of Pharr and Hidalgo, Texas for their support. I thank Araceli Casares, current PCT Board President, all of our board members, and all other supporters for their help. I thank poet and author Seres Jaime Magaña, for agreeing to direct the play in 2018 for PCT. I thank Gabriel H. Sanchez (with Legado Publishing) for this book. And to City of Hidalgo Manager Gonzalez, Mayor Coronado, and City Council for their support and contributions.

And I thank GOD for my many blessings, including family and friendships.

Sincerely,

Co-Author
Pedro Garcia
PCT/Artistic Director/Co-Founder

Author
Lucio G. Rivera

"Tales of the Hidalgo Pumphouse"
A two-act, bilingual play by Lucio G. Rivera and Pedro Garcia, written in 2010

Characters:

Narrator (*A recorded voice over will work. This could very well be the voice of the actor playing Mrs. Stonewall*)

The adults (ranging in ages from 20 to 70)
Mrs. Stonewall
Rufus
Luis
Pala
Riche
Toñita
Woman (optional)
Husband (optional)
Man (optional)

The boys (ranging in age from 9 to 14)
Luisito
Jerry
Nuno
Bandee
Javier

The Girls (ranging in age from 9 -14)
Janie
Mary
Dalia
Rosario
Oralia

_Los Fantasmas/The Creature_s (ranging in age from 18-65)
La Muerte
La Lechuza
La Llorona
El Hombre Sin Cabeza
El Pirata

Hidalgo Pump House Amphitheater and now a Museum!

SETTING: Hidalgo, Texas, Summer of 1972

Up center stage is the interior of a small wooden frame house with a screen door. This is the living area of DON LUIS and DOÑA PAULA "PALA" RIVERA. It consists of a full bed, a dresser, a couple of chairs, a few hanging pictures, a small table and sink and a stove. Down left of the home is an outdoor patio with flowers, plants, shrubbery, several lawn chairs and enough space for dancing, including a platform. Upstage right is the Pumphouse structure and shed and platforms for the working men and las compuertas (these are gates that hold or release the flow of water and where the boys dive from into the water for swimming). There are toolboxes, storages, wooden work horses and lots of tools, both small and large, and an oil can.

The play begins with Mrs. STONEWALL, now 30 years older, as she enters and addresses the audience from down center stage.

ACT ONE: Mrs. Stonewall's introduction

MRS STONEWALL: Hello everyone. I'm Mrs. Stonewall, formerly of the Smithsonian Institution in Washington, DC.

Tonight, we're going to tell you a story that was told to me quite a while back. *(a little absent minded)* Oh wait a minute… *(she checks her notes and chuckles)*.. wrong story. Actually, it's one I started investigating nearly 30 years ago, in the early 1970's, when I first came to visit the old Pumphouse in Hidalgo, Texas when it was still in operations. I ended up visiting so many times that I finally learned to speak some Español. In fact, some of the folks even began to call me Pared de Piedra – that's Stonewall in Spanish. *(she chuckles)* I sure heard some great stories and met some wonderful people.

A large portion of this account is based on fact, and the rest on tales I heard. I embellished quite a bit of course, but hey, don't we all? I mean who's going to believe in fantasmas – that's ghosts and spirits by the way – and about a treasure lost a long time ago by a Pirate named Hidalgo. I tell you; I was skeptical too until I saw for myself.

I call my story "The Miraculous Tales of The Hidalgo Pumphouse", but I cut out "the miraculous" part for short and… well, I don't want to spill all the beans at once, so I'll let you see for yourself how I wrote it down. I'm just going to sit way back there with all of you and see for myself. I sure hope you enjoy this story as much as I enjoyed the experience.

SCENE 1: NUNO ALMOST DROWNS

Outside the Pumphouse shed. Pump house workers RUFUS and LUIS are taking a break.

RUFUS: Did you know that back in 1909 when the Pumphouse was built, it operated with huge steam engines that needed firewood to get started. The fire would create steam pressure to rotate and vacuum the water from the Rio Grande into the canals.

LUIS: Sí, my father and many men cut mesquite trees all along the river and surrounding areas, clearing all the brush to get wood for the fires. They would haul the wood by ox carts. It was very hard work.

RUFUS: I arrived when the Hamilton-Corliss engines were pumping the water much faster as the demand for irrigation grew. We could pump close to 400,000 gallons of water from the river per minute to irrigate all those 72,000 acres of nearby farm crops.

LUIS: In the old days the Pumphouse had two smokestacks.

RUFUS: If it hadn't been for the Hidalgo Pumphouse and the Rio Grande or the invention of the steam engine, this valley would never have been as fertile or prosperous.

There is a long pause as nature sounds of birds and a cool breeze are heard, all is peaceful and beautiful.

LUIS: *(contemplative)* We also attract lots of butterflies and all kinds of birds like the hummingbird, the cardinal and the Calandria.

RUFUS: La Calandria, the Baltimore Oriole.

LUIS: And the snowbirds from up north, they like it here too.

RUFUS: Oh yeah, winter Texans love getting away from the cold and the snow. They like our delicious grapefruit and oranges and our sunny climate.

BOTH: Los Winter Texans. *(they both share a smile)*

RUFUS: Luis let's move those oil barrels before I go up to the house. *(they exit)*

A group of young BOYS enter barefoot and in shorts ready for a cool swim at the Pumphouse canal, the basin. They're playing by the flow gates/las compuertas.

LUISITO: *(shouting as he jumps into the water)* Ayy yai! It feels good!

JERRY: Hey! I can do the same!

JERRY climbs on a concrete column holding las compuertas, then prepares to jump into the canal. BANDEE, who is older and stronger, pushes little NUNO into the water.

NUNO: *(screaming)* Oh no! Wait! I can't swim!

LUISITO: Why did you push him? He can't swim! *(he jumps into the strong current)* Nuno! Dónde estás? Where are you?

JERRY: He's over here!

LUISITO: *(surfacing)* Come on you guys! Quit playing games! Where's my brother?

BANDEE: I thought he could swim. *(he jumps into the water too)*

LUISITO: Jerry! We need to find Nuno! He might drown!

JERRY: No le hagas! Let's go under again!

LUISITO: Bandee! Go get your father Don Rufus or my father Don Luis!

BANDEE runs to get DON LUIS.

BANDEE: *(running)* Don Luis! Don Rufus!

LUIS: *(appearing on the platform with RUFUS close behind)* Pero que tienes, muchacho?!

BANDEE: Nuno fell in the canal and we can't find him!

LUIS: Pero que cosa! *(he drops his tools and races towards las compuertas)*

As DON LUIS runs the distance to save his son, everything seems to go in slow motion (a special effect is captured in time, DON LUIS'S fiery run, the BOYS' anxious search) and we hear the voice of the NARRATOR:

NARRATOR: Don Luis ran as fast as he could, recognizing it was a matter of life or death. He could hear voices from the past saying that the water from the Rio Grande could be blessed or cursed, *(voices)* an omen to some of the folks who drowned in the past. He thought of La Llorona, *(faint cries)* who had been doomed to weep all of her life for drowning her babies. Some of the folks claimed she would come back and take other kids thinking they were hers. As Don Luis ran with all of his might, he prayed *(prayers/chants)* this would not happen to Nuno...

Back to real time.

LUIS: *(as he dives into the water)* Nuno! Nuno! Sal para arriba!

LUISITO: Apa! Aquí! Over here is where Nuno went down!

LUIS: A ver! Maybe he's caught down under las compuertas. *(he submerges like a whale)*

JERRY: Sí! He might have caught his pants on a hook or wire.

LUISITO: Let's all go deep into the current!

LUIS: (coming back up for a breath) Careful! Don't get caught by las corrientes! *(DON LUIS goes under again and grabs the body of NUNO. He yells passionately) Ayy,* muchacho de mi vida, mira como estás!

He jerks him around the chest with his strong arms and miraculously NUNO revives, spitting out water and crying.

NUNO: *(trembling)* Apa! Apa! Tengo miedo!

LUIS: No mi hijo! Don't be afraid! It's okay!

NUNO: Apa, I saw a head of a dead man! It was floating in the water.

LUIS: *(picking up NUNO) Todos* váyanse para la casa. Ándale!

All the BOYS obey and run away. As DON LUIS carries his son to his home, we hear the NARRATOR'S voice:

NARRATOR: Rufus stared from the Pumphouse work shed as Don Luis carried his son home. For many years now, the mighty and benevolent Rufus made sure that the entire Pumphouse functioned properly. He was responsible for pumping out millions of gallons of Rio Grande water into the canals for the important irrigation of the Valley's crops, and he had been witness to a few near drownings before. He broke a grim smile while Don Luis arrived home with his frightened boy.

SCENE 2: THE CURANDERO

LUIS: *(rushing into his home carrying NUNO)* Pala! Pala! Ven pronto!

PALA: *(appearing from the washroom where she had been doing the laundry)* Sí, Luis, qué pasó?

LUIS: Bring me a towel and a cup of yerba buena tea, pronto!

PALA: Sí, Luis, ya voy! Pero qué le pasó a Nuno?! *(she grabs a cup of tea from the stove)*

LUIS: Este muchacho se cayó al canal. No hace caso.

LUISITO appears and stands by the screen door.

LUISITO: Sí, Ama, he almost drowned.

PALA: *(hysterical)* Por eso les digo que no anden jugando en el canal! Do you understand me?! I don't want to see you around el canal without a grown up!

14

LUIS: Estos muchachos are too hardheaded.

PALA: There's something wrong with this boy, Luis.

LUIS: Mujer! Didn't I tell you, he almost drowned! He's scared.

NUNO: Sí, Ama, I saw the floating head of a dead man!

PALA: Que dead man que ni tus patas! Mi pobre muchacho! Don't cry anymore. (beat) Luisito, call your Tío Riche para que lo venga curar del susto! Córrale, muchacho! *(he speeds off)*

LUIS: Take care of him, vieja, I have to go back to La Pompa. I'll return soon.

NUNO: No, Apa!

PALA: Mijito, don't be afraid! Everything is going to be fine.

NUNO: Uuyyyy Ama, tengo miedo!

PALA: No, mi hijo! No tengas miedo! I'm here to protect you.

RICHE arrives with a small tree branch with lots of leaves and a short-handled broom.

PALA: It's good you come over, Riche.

RICHE: *(studying NUNO closely)* Let's see, lay him down on the table.

PALA: Dice que vio la cabeza de un muerto en el agua del canal. Pobre mijo, por poco se ahoga, pero Dios es muy grande. Mira, parece que trae calentura. No vuelvas ir al canal, Nuno. No vuelvas jamás!

NUNO: No, Ama, no vuelvo ir!

RICHE and PALA begin their ritual curanderismo de susto.

PALA: Todo espíritu y demonios departen de este muchachito.

RICHE: En el nombre del Espíritu Santo y Padre todo poderoso, les ordeno espíritus malos que se alejen de este muchacho y que se vayan para los campos secos donde nadie vive. Váyanse en el nombre de Jesús!

NUNO: *(crying loudly) No*! No! No! It hurts!

From up center stage a HEADLESS MAN appears to hover over the ritual with howling wind sounds. He seems to be struggling, unseen by the trio. A mystic music underscores this scene.

PALA: *(she sweeps NUNO's body with a tree branch)* *Cállate*, muchacho! Come out evil spirit of fear! Huyan, espíritus del mal!

RICHE: *(lifting his arms) Sálganse*, espíritus malos del demonio! Salgan y nunca vuelvan! *(he sweeps the tree branch lightly over NUNO's trembling body. The HEADLESS SPIRIT, defeated, leaves and the wind and howling vanish)*

NUNO falls into a deep sleep.

RICHE: Ya salieron los espíritus malos que este muchacho traía.

PALA: Mi hijo! Everything is okay now! Dios te cuide!

The lights fade.

SCENE 3: A STRANGE OCCURRENCE

LUIS and RUFUS are working on the pump engine. LUIS hands RUFUS the oil can to squirt the bolts of the motor.

RUFUS: Gracias. How is your son doing?

LUIS: He's ok now, but he was scared to death.

RUFUS: I tell you Luis, throughout the years that you and I have worked these pumps many things have happened, things we can't even explain. I done told Jerry not to be messing around the canal.

A clinking sound of a falling wrench is heard, and a group of pigeons fly away in desperation from the roof.

LUIS: What was that?

RUFUS: *(glancing up towards the roof)* It's only some birds trying to set up their nests. I hear there's a hurricane coming out of the Gulf of Mexico.

17

LUIS: I don't know, but I think those birds are being haunted by something else.

RUFUS: You may be right. *(the wind howls again and the HEADLESS MAN'S shadow appears looking from the window unseen by the two. He moves the oil can)* I feel cold. Mira, Luis, the window! *(the shadow disappears)*

LUIS: Dónde?

RUFUS: It's gone already, but I smell sulfur and a dead odor.

LUIS: I smell it too.

RUFUS: That's what I'm talking about. Something's just not right. These strange happenings have been going on for a long time now.

LUIS: *(the pigeons fly off again) There* go the pigeons again. They see something we don't see.

RUFUS: Maybe es El Diablo o La Muerte!

LUIS: Maria Purísima! Don't say that! Eso dijo Nuno, que vió La Muerte.

RUFUS: It could be que La Muerte y El Diablo andan sueltos, you know, looking for somebody to take with them.

LUIS: Or it could be El Hombre Sin Cabeza.

RUFUS: Maybe.

18

LUIS: Say Rufus, did you get the oil can that was right here?

RUFUS: No, hombre, I gave it to you.

LUIS: Rufus, how did it get up there? I didn't put it there.

RUFUS: Me neither. *(more chilling sounds are heard) Luis*! Vámonos! Something's not right. *(they scurry out)*

The HEADLESS MAN appears on the platform with the oil can. He dances to some chilling ancient music. He's mystical and a touch humorous as well.

As the lights change the NARRATOR is heard.

NARRATOR: The moon was shining brightly upon the Southern point of Texas and its borderline with Mexico. Many folks around the area still shared some of their ancient ancestors' beliefs that the full moon had special supernatural powers, where evil spirits and werewolves… and the headless singer of course… *(the HEADLESS MANN takes a bow)* would come out to haunt the people, seeking souls to take back to their dark world. Others believed in hidden treasures along the river guided by a mysterious shining light.

Lights fade.

SCENE 4: TURN IN FOR THE NIGHT

DON LUIS, tired after a hard day's work, comes home where his wife PALA is in her robe kneeling to pray. He

*only takes off his shoes and over-shirt and gets into bed.
After a moment PALA joins him.*

LUIS: How beautiful the full moon appears through the window, eh, vieja?

PALA: Sí, viejo, but I smell a dead odor.

LUIS: No serán tus patas?

PALA: Ayy Luis, cállate. Lo digo en serio.

LUIS: Sí, Rufus and I smelled the same thing en La Pompa earlier. Rufus claims he saw a black shadow… then it disappeared leaving a strong olor de muerto.

PALA: Ayyy Luis! Puede ser El Diablo! Aay, Maria Purísima! *(she reaches for the bed sheet and covers both herself and LUIS entirely)* Es algo malo!

LUIS: Como decía mi abuelita Irene, anda El Diablo suelto!

The HEADLESS MAN appears again peeking through the window. PALA and LUIS under the covers do not see him. Eerie sounds are heard again.

PALA: Ayy, Maria Purísima, Holy mother of God! No digas eso, Luis. *(they embrace tightly. Suddenly a large fart is heard from under the covers)*

BOTH: *(simultaneously)* LUIS/PALA! *(uncovering themselves and scaring off the offended HEADLESS MAN)*

LUIS: Yo no fui!

PALA: Yo tampoco.

LUIS: A la mejor fue el fantasma.

Offstage we hear the fantasma:

EL HOMBRE SIN CABEZA: Tampoco fui yo!

LUIS: What was that?

PALA: *(grabbing a cross from under her pillow) Whatever* it is, it's not coming in here! *(after a moment's pause, the wind blows, a faraway dog barks and rain begins)*
LUIS: I think a storm is coming, vieja. *(suddenly loud thunder is heard and they both yell, covering themselves all the way again)*

Lights out.

SCENE 5: THE SCHOOL PROJECT

The next day, several neighborhood GIRLS, including DALIA who is Don Luis's daughter, are playing a game of jacks and patty cakes. They are sitting on the platform in the patio next to Pala's home. None of the boys are present. Beautiful music starts the scene.

JANIE: We all need to get started on our school project if we want to get a good grade.

MARY: But it's boring in Mrs. Baker's history class. I can't stand it.

DALIA: Me either, Mrs. Baker slapped me in the back for speaking Spanish as I was going out of the room.

ROSARIO: Well, at least you didn't get three swats, like Pepe did for laughing out loud in Mr. Garza's room. Anyways, that kind of punishment will probably stop in the future.

DALIA: Yes, my mother says that's cruel and unusual punishment and that the school should change its rules.

ROSARIO: Look, we'll all work together and get this school report ready so we can get a good grade. Janie will be our leader and director.

JANIE: Okay, the five of us will research the old Pumphouse for the book report and also choreograph the dance for the festival in honor of the Rio Grande. I brought a book about steam engines. Where's Oralia? She's late.

DALIA: I brought one on the history of the Pumphouse and its use for irrigation. It all started in the early 1900's and the Pumphouse was opened in exactly 1909.

ROSARIO: My great grandfather Bartolo used to work at La Pompa. He once told me that he carried mesquite wood on his ox cart for the fire that produced the steam to run the pumps. (*all the girls stare at her wide eyed*)

JANIE: That's real good, Rosario! Let's write that down!

DALIA: Yes, and my Tío Luis made sure the boilers were hot enough to do their work and Mr. Huerta made sure all the machine parts were oiled all the time. And Mr. Wisdom... well... he was the boss.

MARY: Remember, Mrs. Baker also wants us to write about the inventor of the steam engines.

JANIE: (*taking notes*) Oh, I know! He was a very intelligent Scottish man named James Watt born in 1736. He liked learning a lot as a young man. I only wish some of the boys around here were like him.

ROSARIO: That would be a miracle. But that's good history. And remember we also have to write about the water from the Rio Grande and why it was pumped.

MARY: Oh, I know. I wrote something about it. *(she stands and clears her throat and starts reading)* The Pump House was built in 1909 by the Louisiana-Rio Grande Canal Company that was partly owned by Mr. Pharr and Mr. Kelly who were farming and living in Pharr, Texas, and by a Mr. Closner. These men wanted to advance the process of water irrigation for the mass production of crops like sugar cane, cotton, cabbage, lettuce, watermelons, oranges and lots of tomatoes, and chili peppers!

DALIA: Oh, I love chili peppers! *(everybody giggles)*

JANIE: That's great information! But we're gonna need to expand the report to include how the Rio Grande Valley's agriculture affects the rest of the country. Oh, and on the importance of the railroad for shipping. I know we'll get good grades!

ROSARIO: There were also strange things happening back then. My Grandpa used to talk about the huge hurricane that flooded all of Hidalgo in the 30's that changed the direction of the river. He said they had to dig out the big channel on the west side of the Pumphouse to make sure the water still made it to the pumps. *(pause) He* also said that La Llorona, El Hombre Sin Cabeza and La Lechuza would often appear.

MARY: I love spooky stories...

JANIE: Ok, ok, chavalonas, enough about La Llorona. Let's practice our dance for the blessing of the Rio Grande and the crops.

The GIRLS position themselves and insert an 8-track tape into a music box. The music starts and they begin a dance that resembles the Matachín movements of old Mexico. JANIE is the lead. Soon they are all in perfect unison and doing very well. After a few minutes they stop.

JANIE: Muy bien...muy bien! You're catching on perfectly. Our book report and dance will be the best. *(they all laugh)*

ROSARIO: I wonder why boys don't do as well as girls and yet they always think they do.

MARY: My mom says it's pride. Like my father, for instance... at home he always asks my mom for advice on how to do things, but he wouldn't dare ask her outside the house.

DALIA: One day I hope the boys are nice to us girls. *(a silent moment pondering the last comment)*
JANIE: We could ask them to help us with the report and the dance.

Suddenly a little girl named ORALIA appears from nowhere, startling the GIRLS, pretending she's la llorona (the weeping woman).

ORALIA: Mis hijas! (they scream) I scared you! Ha, ha, ha, ha! (beat) Did you hear about Nuno almost drowning yesterday? He said he saw El Hombre Sin Cabeza y La Llorona.

ROSARIO: Oh yeah, where is he now?

ORALIA: He went with the boys to Tejano lake to search for a treasure.

All the GIRLS stop and stare and make incredulous gestures. Then they pick up their stuff and run off.

ORALIA: Hey, wait for me! *(she runs off)*

Lights out.

SCENE 6: THE BOYS ON THE LEVEE

LUISITO and the BOYS decided to walk up towards Tejano Lake. They were looking for another place to hang out and go swimming and where they could play tag and hide 'n' go seek or canoe in the water. They came upon a wooded patch that surrounded an abandoned irrigation canal.

LUISITO: (*standing at the top of the levee of the empty irrigation canal*) This levee we walk on is where the sheriff herded his cows all across town to pasture and back. The now empty canal used to be full of water. It flowed from the river to the lake and to Pate and Kencho's fields.

JERRY: And what happened? Where are the cows and the water?

BANDEE: Times change, boy. Maybe it was cursed.

LUISITO: Coulda been. But you know, the water from el Rio Grande starts in the San Juan Mountains of Colorado all the way down through New Mexico, bending in El Paso and flowing out into the Gulf of Mexico.

JAVIER: That's why some people think the water is blessed.

JERRY: Yeah, almost 1,900 miles long, also dividing Mexico and the United States.

LUISITO: El Rio Grande, or el Rio Bravo as it's known in old Mexico, is joined by El Rio Conchos before it empties into the Gulf.

NUNO: You're really smart, Luisito. I don't know why the girls think we're stupid. (*they ignore him*)

JAVIER: The flowing fresh water from the Rockies and Sierra Madre bring life to this area and to Mexico too.

BANDEE: My father said if it wasn't for El Rio, we wouldn't be living here, none of us. But who cursed it and why?

LUISITO: Well, that's a good question. But it also goes back to the times of los Españoles y los Piratas.

NUNO: (*excited*) The Hidalgo Pirates?

JAVIER: No! Not the football team, stupid, real pirates! How'd they get here?

JERRY: The Conquistadores and the Pirates used to sail from across the ocean to the Gulf of Mexico, and like my father says, they had a lot of gold and treasures, but some died and got killed when they were ship wrecked by the coast, around Corpus Christi and South Padre Island. That's when they left their treasures behind.

LUISITO: They say los fantasmas del Rio Grande took their tesoros! That's how come the river can be cursed, with La Llorona, La Lechuza y La Muerte.

JERRY: Y El Hombre Sin Cabeza! (h*e opens his arms and makes a scary face. They shriek*)

BANDEE: Quiet! Cut it out!

LUISITO: Come on, you guys. Tomorrow we'll go to the Pumphouse pits where the big engines are. The fantasmas meet there. We'll spy on them to find out where the treasure is buried, so we can strike it rich with tons of diamonds and gold chains! Mañana, boys, mañana.

As he mimics holding lots of gold chains, a noise of shaking tree branches, voices and some footsteps are heard nearby. The black shadow of LA MUERTE is staring at them from the distance, but they cannot see him. A flock of small birds fly away. A baby is heard crying.

JERRY: I hear somebody in the woods.

NUNO: I hear a baby. Quiero a mi ama.

LUISITO: Shhh! Sea hombre, Nuno!

JERRY: Some people who live around here say the lake is also cursed because they found a dead baby lying in the bamboos.

NUNO: Maybe it belonged to La Llorona.

BANDEE: Maybe we ought to forget about this and go home!

More footsteps are heard but louder this time, as LA MUERTE moves in closer. A wailing cry of LA LLORONA is heard as she appears. Then LA LECHUZA approaches. There is thunder in the distance and flickering lighting only allowing glimpses of the creatures and their outstretched arms and shiny fangs. The BOYS release a loud shrieking yell and turn and run as fast they can towards their houses.

Lights out.

SCENE 7: JANIE'S DREAM

The girls are back on the platform by Pala's patio.

ROSARIO: My tía tells the best stories in the world.

DALIA: Yeah, and she also makes the best raspas too.

MARY: You think the boys might want to play a game of Red Rover Red Rover tonight?

JANIE: I bet you want to hold hands with Luisito.

MARY: No, I don't, but I know *you* do!

ROSARIO: Don't worry, boys don't like girls. They only like to scare us; they're only interested in hidden treasures and fantasmas.

ORALIA: I saw La Llorona once.

DALIA: No, you didn't.

JANIE: Yeah, she did, it was the night when your tía told the story of El Hombre Sin Cabeza who lost his head in a jealous rage because another man looked at his wife.

ORALIA: It was chopped off with a machete at the sugar cane field on the old military highway in San Juan.

Unknown to the GIRLS, the HEADLESS MAN appears in the distance. He's enjoying the tale about him. He strums a Spanish classical tune on his guitar to underscore the recounting of the story.

ROSARIO: Tell us what happened.

As ORALIA begins the story, it's reenacted by two MEN and a WOMAN. (reenacting is optional)

ORALIA: The two men were sugar cane workers, cutting long stalks with their machetes and were very thirsty. Along came one man's wife with drinking water for her husband.

The re-enactors appear on stage, two young men and a young woman.

ORALIA: As she approached her husband, she dropped the water cup, the other man fixed his eyes on her…

WOMAN: Ayy Juan, se cayó el vaso.

The beautiful WOMAN picks up the cup as the other MAN admires her.

HUSBAND: (*Upset*) Oye, tú, que miras?

MAN: La vista es muy natural.

HUSBAND: (*offended*) No me gusta como miras a mi esposa. Defiéndete o te mueres.

The two men fence with their machetes as the fearful woman watches.

ORALIA: The two men fought for hours, and right at midnight, one of them lost his head in the heated battle in the middle of the sugarcane field under the full moon. They say every full moon at midnight you can hear a man cutting cane searching for his lost head on Military Road deep en los cañaverales.

The battle stops and the three reinactors exit.

The HEADLESS MAN sets down his guitar and walks over to the GIRLS.

EL HOMBRE SIN CABEZA: Excuse me, ladies. (*startled, they freeze and scream as he bows*) Would any of you care to dance?

JANIE takes the offer and they both dance a macabre waltz. After a moment the GIRLS and the HEADLESS MAN slip off, leaving Janie twirling by herself. She lies on a bed brought on stage. The music is louder. After a moment, she wakes with a scream! TONITA enters and sits by her.

TONITA: Niña, ese grito… You had a bad dream, mija.

JANIE: Ayy, Mama. I was dancing with El Hombre Sin Cabeza.

TONITA: Was he handsome? (smiling)

JANIE: I don't know, Mama, he was headless!
TONITA: But mija, I told you many times that those are only stories made up to scare you kids into being good. Now get some rest and I'll bring you some te de manzanilla.

EL HOMBRE SIN CABEZA re-enters before TONITA can move.

31

EL HOMBRE SIN CABEZA: Don't worry, I'll get it.

They both scream as the lights go out. Loud laughter is heard in the dark.

SCENE 8: RUFUS & LUIS GO FISHING

RUFUS and LUIS are taking a break and fishing at the Pumphouse, drinking lemonade and talking about work and the old days.

RUFUS: Time sure passes by, Luis. Now the pumps run with natural gas and soon they will move down river and operate on electricity, so I've heard.

LUIS: It will never be the same. These old engines have been operating and making lots of noise since La Pompa opened in the early nineteen hundreds. La Pompa es el Corazón de Hidalgo, like a heartbeat that provides life.

RUFUS: You're a philosopher Luis. *(pause)* Do you remember el guero Sweet? He said he could hear the hissing and clanking sounds miles away. He could see the smoke from his home in Reynosa. I don't know how he got here. I never asked, but he was good at his job. Y tú también eres muy bueno, Luis.

LUIS: Thank you, Rufus. You too are a very smart mayordomo. There is nobody better than you to run the pumps. Who else was there, back then?

RUFUS: Well let's see. There was Chester Possum, Bob Possum, Peter Bosch and then there was Billy Moore right when I got here. Gus Champion was foreman.

LUIS: That's right, and the Hidalgo Irrigation District Number Two has controlled the Pumphouse and its irrigation canals since 1920. That's where we still get our pay checks para el numero social. (*they share a laugh*)

LUIS: Did you talk to that nice woman who came looking for you yesterday?

RUFUS: Sure did. Her name is Mrs. Stonewall. She's the one who got me thinking about this old pump being more important than just my job. Turns out she's an archivist with the Smithsonian in Washington and she's documenting the history of agriculture in the Rio Grande Valley. She wants to know all about La Pompa for the future. Nice lady, although she talks a bunch, almost made me forgot to check the boiler temperature. I sure don't want no explosions. She took lots of notes and said she'd be back.

Suddenly voices and running feet are heard in the distance followed by lightning and thunder. RUFUS and LUIS stretch their necks to catch a glimpse of a small GROUP OF PEOPLE scurrying past.

LUIS: Son mojados. Siempre pasan por aquí. Ya hicieron su camino.

RUFUS: Pobrecitos. I hear that the Border Patrol or el gobierno Americano someday will build a huge wall by the Rio so they can't cross anymore.

LUIS: No creo. They'll always find a way to cross and find jobs. After all, all of this land used to belong to Spain and Mexico at one time. At least until Mexican General Santa Ana lost the land to General Sam Houston making him sign property papers around 1846.

RUFUS: You sure know your history, Luis.

LUIS: My daughter and her friends teach me when I hear them practicing. They're also writing a history of La Pompa. Would you believe it Rufus, one day you and I are gonna be famous! *(they share a laugh as LUIS gets a bite on the line)*

LUIS: 'Stán picando!

RUFUS: You got a bite!

BOTH: Jálale, jálale!!!

There is a big splash and a happy tune as lights fade.

SCENE 9: SPYING ON THE FANTASMAS

Los FANTASMAS are having a meeting down in the dark pits of La Pompa to decide where to hide their huge treasure chest. The BOYS sneak up looking down at them from high above on the platform near the nesting pigeons. As terrified as they are, their mission is to locate the fantasmas's treasure hideout. A hideous but subtle macabre score underlines the chilling scene.

LA MUERTE: Yo soy El Rey of the dark world. Those who come to me will stay for eternal life in my dungeons.

LA LECHUZA: Shreeiiillll, Shhreeiiilll, Schhreeeiiilll!
(she releases a high-pitched whistling cry)

LA LLORONA: Ayeee! Oooeee! Mis hijos! *(wails)*

LA MUERTE: Ya nos encontramos otra vez!
Necesitamos más almas y buscar un lugar para esconder el tesoro!

The BOYS stare in disbelief and shock. They can hardly breathe as they stare in horror down at los FANTASMAS and the treasure box now open.

LUISITO: Wow! There's a lot of gold and diamonds down there to make all of us rich!

JERRY: You're right! But how are we going to take it without fighting them?

BANDEE: It's not going to be easy.

LUISITO: We'll have to catch them off guard!

BANDEE: All of this gold and diamonds from the dead is the root of all evil.

NUNO: We should get going! If they find us here, that's it for us.

LUISITO: Shhh! We need to hear where they're hiding the treasure box, so we can go after it.

LA MUERTE points his three forked fingers at each of LOS FANTASMAS and towards the gold and the jewelry spilling over the treasure chest. They greet him with open arms and bow to him slowly, showing their loyalty.

LA MUERTE: Es bueno vernos de vuelta! Necesitamos más almas! *(voice trembles as he speaks with authority and command)* Quiero más almas y oro! Y cuerpos en el camposanto! Jaaa! Jaaa! Jaaa! *(displays his blood-stained teeth while lifting his arms and releases a crackling laugh)*

LA LLORONA: Ya vendrán más! Jajajaja!!!!

EL HOMBRE SIN CABEZA: *(speaks from his heart)* **Es** verdad, mi General y Jefe, we'll bring more souls and gold into our dark world.

LA MUERTE: Hiss! Hiss! Hiss! That's what I like to hear! Talking from the heart is like poetry and not lies!

LA MUERTE'S voice trembles as he spits another flame of red fire up into the air and towards the BOYS' direction.

LUISITO: Wow! He's like a dragon!

JAVIER: Like a serpent! And it's looking up towards us!

NUNO: We need to go!

JERRY: We can't move, or they'll see us. *(motions with his hands for the rest to remain silent)*

LA LECHUZA: *(releases her shrieking whistling noise)* Shhhhrriiiieeeeeelll!

The BOYS jump closer to each other and freeze. They are petrified, their eyes wide with fear.

EL HOMBRE SIN CABEZA: I must say, those who have done wrong in their lives will now be ours forever. Ja! Ja! Ja!

LA LECHUZA: Si! Tienes razón! Nobody will save them from our dark world and burning infierno! Y Usted, Doña Llorona, porqué está tan triste? Soon you will have more and more hijos to take care of. Ja! Ja! Ja!

LA LLORONA: No es eso! No estoy triste! Pero siento lástima por mis hijos que se ahogaron en El Rio! Ayyy, mis hijos! Mis hijos…Eeeeh! Eeeeh! *(she releases a deep painful moan)*

LA LECHUZA: Shhhrrriiiiieeeeelll!

LA MUERTE: No llore, Llorona. *(moving closer, he places a skeletal arm around her, displaying bloody teeth and a broken skull, then releases a loud screech)* Jaaaaa! Jaaaa! Estamos en el mundo de los muertos!

NUNO: *(covering his eyes)* Tengo miedo! I want to go home! *(he cries out quietly)*

BANDEE: Yo también! I don't want to be here anymore!

LUISITO: Okay you guys, we'll make our way home as soon as the fantasmas say where they'll hide the treasure. It has to be ours.

LA MUERTE: Remember! Recuerden... Quiero este tesoro enterrado en lo profundo del camposanto viejo de Hidalgo. Me entienden?! *(lifting up his hands with gold chains and diamond rings, he releases more flames of fire through his snout)* Es de nosotros! Y nadie no lo va quitar! Nunca! Nunca!

LUISITO: *(in a low voice)* Listen! They're gonna bury the treasure at the old Hidalgo cemetery.

JAVIER: Shhh! They're saying something else!

EL HOMBRE SIN CABEZA: Si, mi Jefe! I want to go to el camposanto, it's my favorite place!

LA MUERTE: I hold the keys to el camposanto y el mundo del infierno! Nobody will come near our tesoro!

LA LLORONA: Yo los llevaré por el camino al viejo panteón, síganme.

LA MUERTE points his long-clawed hands at the jewels that have fallen from the treasure box. They quickly get placed back into the box. The lid is closed with a loud thump and locked with two heavy padlocks as they begin to drag it up the stairway.

JERRY: Wow! They got special magic power!

LUISITO: It's black magic!

BANDEE: They got power! But we need to get out of here!

As the BOYS are whispering, LA MUERTE hears them and glances up towards them.

LA MUERTE: Oigan! Listen! I heard somebody up there!

LA LECHUZA: Whoever it might be will be ours! Shreiiiiellll!

LA LECHUZA'S cries cause the pigeons to fly away wildly; dogs can be heard barking as the wind begins to howl and the music gets louder.

LUISITO: (*shouting*) Let's go! The fantasmas are heading out!

LUISITO gets a hold of JERRY'S arm and pulls him. The rest of the BOYS follow, and as soon as they hit the floor, they run as fast as they can down the levee and away from los FANTASMAS. Lights out.

SCENE 10: LAS ENCHILADAS

RUFUS and LUIS are sitting outside.

LUIS: Rufus, it's good you to come visit and eat with us. Ahorita están las enchiladas. How come your wife didn't come?

RUFUS: She's busy baking three peach pies but sends her regards. She's gonna send one later.

LUIS: 'Ta bueno, you'll take her a plate of Pala's delicious enchiladas when you go home.

RUFUS: That'll be fine. *(beat)* **My** son was telling me something about a buried treasure and evil spirits, have you heard anything?

LUIS: These kids tienen El Diablo metido. They're spooked from the stories they hear. My sister-in-law Gabriela is a good storyteller.

RUFUS: That may be, but sometimes I believe there are ghosts and creepy creatures around the pumps and the river. Don't you? *(a dog barks loudly off stage before LUIS can answer and a WOMAN yells)*

TONITA: *(offstage)* Perro mugroso, váyase de aquí! Ándele… shhhhhttaaaaa!

LUIS: *(without moving)* Blacky, placate boy! *(the dog settles down)*

TONITA, a middle-aged woman with a slight hunchback wearing a scarf, enters and greets the MEN.

TONITA: Oye Luis, Rufus! Ese perro se me hace que tiene la rabia! Porque no lo amarras?

LUIS: No te hace nada, mujer. Yo creo que piensa que eres La Llorona. *(he laughs, but she doesn't find it amusing)* Allí está Pala adentro, pásale.

TONITA continues into the house offstage to join PALA in the kitchen.

RUFUS: What do you think, Luis?

LUIS: De que estábamos hablando?

RUFUS: De los fantasmas.

LUIS: Oh sí! Sometimes I get confused with all the noise at the Pumphouse. I think I can hear the voices of the old workers. And with all the heat and humidity down in the pits, it gets rough.

RUFUS: It's amazing how we can stand all that heat and noise. So many years now…

LUIS: I started working at La Pompa in 1928 when I was 17 years old. I made a dollar a day. My father who was there from the beginning was making $1.25, just enough to survive. He got me started. But I have this home loaned to me from the company. La Pompa is all the work I've ever known for nearly 50 years.

RUFUS: I came along in 1943 right after Pearl Harbor. I started on the dredge boat cleaning the channel, then moved up to the Pumphouse as foreman.

LUIS: In all that time I've seen La Llorona maybe twice. I could swear I saw her with my own eyes. Once it was by the old Ingersoll down in the pits. She was sitting there crying when I was gonna oil the machine. After I closed my eyes a couple of times she was gone. I was scared.

41

RUFUS: I saw her once too. She was grabbing peaches one-night form my giant trees. She was wearing a long white dress with a veil and long black hair.

LUIS: Yeah, that's how I saw her too.

RUFUS: She wasn't scary looking or anything. I could hardly make out her face, a pale powdery white, but she gave me the creeps. I went to get my wife, but then she was gone.

TONITA enters with two glasses of ice-cold lemonade for the men.

BOTH: Gracias.

LUIS: Come on, Rufus, I want to show you that new rooster that hatched a few weeks ago. His daddy was a chachalaca!

RUFUS: You don't say!

LUIS: Yea, I'll show you. Tonita, dile a Pala que ya vamos a comer!

The MEN exit and PALA enters wearing an apron, dusting her hands.

PALA: Dónde se fue Luis y Rufus?

TONITA: A ver el gallo de la chachalaca.

PALA: Ahh, sí.

TONITA: Como te decía, Pala, la casa de corte estaba aquí en Hidalgo primero y también la cárcel, pero las movieron pa' Edinburgo después del gran aguacero, el flood.

PALA: Adio!

TONITA: También allí en la cárcel colgaban a los prisioneros y a uno de ellos le cortaron la cabeza, y dicen que en la noche se paraba en la ventana a buscarla.

PALA: A buscar a quién?

TONITA: Pues a su cabeza, que no me 'stas oyendo, mujer?

PALA: Ayy, Tonita, es que entre tú y mi hermana cuentan tantos cuentos que ya hasta los huercos se los creen.

LA LECHUZA flies by unseen by both, making her shrill cry.

TONITA: *(quickly turns her head)* Ayy, Maria Purísima… hay pasó La Lechuza. No la mires, ni le grites porque te escupe cosa blanca y te quedas temblando.

PALA: Como es eso? *(tries not to laugh)*

TONITA: No te rías. Así le pasó a Chicho. Una noche andaba jugando a las escondidas con los huercos y pasó la lechuza, y este le gritó, ALLÍ VA LA BRUJA! Y que se devuelve, y le vomita la cosa blanca. Nunca quedó igual, el pobre huerco. Dicen que le dan unos temblores por todo el cuerpo, así mira. *(she trembles all over as though having a seizure. PALA is laughing)*

TONITA: Sigue riéndote y te va a pasar a tí. *(she sees something move offstage)* Qué fue eso? Algo se movió en aquél canasto, Pala.

PALA: Ahh, de ser el gato. *(she laughs)*

TONITA: No te rías, mujer, que los fantasmas andan sueltos y por eso vamos a rezar el Rosario al rato que lleguen aquellas.

PALA: Pues anda avísales que se vengan a la noche, y de pasada dile a Luis que entren a comer enchiladas. Ándale, apúrate, mujer!

TONITA: 'Ta bueno. *(they exit in different directions)*

PALA: *(yells offstage)* Cuidado con La Llorona!

TONITA: *(offstage)* Sígale!

Lights out with fun music.

SCENE 11: A DUET WITH JANIE

The GIRLS are jumping rope and playing patty cakes as TONITA walks hurriedly across the stage. The GIRLS stop playing.

ALL OF THEM: Hi, Tía Tonita...

TONITA: *(suddenly notices they are there)* *Qué* están haciendo?

ALL: Estamos jugando!

TONITA: Bueno, pórtense bien.

ALL: Ok, we will!

TONITA: *(as is going offstage)* *Y* no me hablen pa trás!

ALL: Ok, we won't! *(she exits)*

ROSARIO: Who do you think is a better storyteller, Tía Tonita or Tía Gabriela?

DALIA: I like them both.

ORALIA: Yeah, they tell the stories differently.

JANIE: Ok! What more have we come up with for the Pumphouse project?

MARY: I have the most important information of all!
ALL OF THEM: Oh yeah?

MARY: If you had to think really hard, what would you say was the main reason for the Pumphouse?

ORALIA: That's easy: to pump water from the Rio Grande.

MARY: But why?

ROSARIO: For plants, vegetables… crops!

JANIE: For animals like cows and goats.

DALIA: For chickens and birdies too.

ORALIA: And for rabbits and turkeys.

ROSARIO: Oh, and for our drinking and bathing and cleaning water, most importantly.

MARY: Listen! Water from our pumps also helped the citrus industry flourish with major cash crops like oranges, grapefruits, lemons, limes, tangerines, and hybrids such as tangelos, which are a cross between a tangerine and an orange.

ORALIA: That girl is smart.

JANIE: Our valley grapefruits are the pinkest and the most delicious from anywhere in the world, as far as I'm concerned.

DALIA: I have something to add.

ALL: What?

DALIA: The railroad! Did you know that the nearby city of Pharr had the main railroad depot, also known as the Hub, with connections to the rest of the country at the corner of US Highway 281, The Pan American Freeway, and Highway 83? From that point trains were loaded with citrus and other vegetables for shipping all over the USA and the world. *(the other GIRLS are speechless and after a*

46

pause, DALIA acknowledges and continues) That's all I have to say.

ALL:

1. That's mighty fine.
2. A miracle.
3. Oranges and grapefruits.
4. Trains.
5. The Pumphouse.

ALL: That's amazing!

JANIE: Now all we need is a short description of the pumps and the engines.

MARY: And practice the dance.

ROSARIO: How about the song? Luisito is a good singer.

ORALIA: Maybe he can sing with Janie.

DALIA: That's crazy, he'll never do it.

MARY: Yes, he will.

ORALIA: *(teasing)* He'll do *anything* for *Janie*.

All the GIRLS go "oooooooohhh" rubbing their fingers and saying "Shane, shane, shane..."

ALL: Janie's gonna marry Luisito... Janie's gonna marry Luisito!

JANIE: No, I'm not! *(she chases the GIRLS off stage)*

Lights out.

SCENE 12: LUISITO MEETS THE PIRATE

The BOYS and GIRLS are playing a game of Red Rover Red Rover on the street near the Pumphouse. It is close to dusk and the sky is orange and purple.

BANDEE: Red Rover, Red Rover, let Oralia come over!

ORALIA runs over and doesn't break the line and has to join the BOYS' side.

ORALIA: Luisito, do you like Janie?

LUISITO: What?

ORALIA: She wants you to sing with her for the talent show and book report. Will you do it?

LUISITO: No!

It's the GIRLS' turn to call someone over.

ROSARIO: Red Rover, Red Rover, let Luisito come over.

He runs over between JANIE and ROSARIO and doesn't break the line and ends up holding hands with JANIE.

ROSARIO: Janie wants to ask you something.

JANIE: No, I don't!

DALIA: Come on, ask him.

JANIE: Oh, ok. Will you sing a song with me for the talent show?

LUISITO: *(he looks over towards the BOYS)* I don't know, what would the boys say?

MARY: It's not like you're gonna *marry* her.

JANIE: It's ok if you don't want to, but you sing nice in church.

LUISITO: Ok... I'll...

An ADULT shouts from off stage and LUISITO does not get to finish his thought.

ADULT: Vénganse huercos, que es tiempo del cuento! Vénganse!

JANIE: Thanks! We're gonna sing beautiful, you'll see. *(she runs off with the other kids)*

LUISITO: But wait, I was gonna say I'd think about it... wait a minute!

He's left onstage by himself. DON RICHE (in his 70's) enters humming a tune on his way to work at the pump. He doesn't see LUISITO.

LUISITO: Don Riche!

RICHE: *(startled, making fun karate movements)* Ayy, Diosito Santo, Maria Purísima! Quién anda hay?

LUISITO: It's me, Luisito.

RICHE: Pero what's the matter with you, muchacho, do you want to give me a heart attack? I could've killed you.

LUISITO: I'm sorry, Don Riche, but I want to ask you a question. Do you believe in los fantasmas and their hidden treasures?

RICHE: When I was a boy, my abuelo said he saw a Spanish pirate by the riverbank with a fast sword. He was chasing La Muerte and a few other fantasmas who had taken his treasure.

LUISITO: A pirate?

RICHE: He was very brave, but the fantasmas overpowered him and rode off with the jewels on big black horses. My abuelo said the treasure was hidden in the Pumphouse pits.

LUISITO: So, it's true!

RICHE: Que dices?

LUISITO: I've seen the fantasmas, and I know where they will hide the treasure next, but I need the pirate. Where can I find him?

RICHE: I've only seen him in my dreams. Allí lo encuentras, en tus sueños. *(realizing the time)* Es tarde!

Tengo que trabajar la noche en La Pompa. Vete pa' la casa, muchacho, no te vaya agarrar por aquí La Lechuza. *(RICHE runs out leaving LUISITO alone)*

The stage becomes darker as the fluorescent LECHUZA (the big white owl) appears flying by with her shrill cry. LUISITO hides as she lands to inspect the area. Then she motions to the other FANTASMAS that the coast is clear. They drag a treasure chest followed by the guitar-playing HEADLESS MAN. They stop for a rest as the HEADLESS MAN crescendos his spicy flamenco tune. It ends and he takes a bow.

LA MUERTE: Tocas muy bien, descabezado, con el alma de los muertos…jajajajajaja!

LA LLORONA slowly walks downstage as though searching for her lost children. Her voice is soft, sorrowful and poetic.

LA LLORONA: Ayyy… Ayyy… Noche de mi mal… estrellas que iluminan mi destrucción. Salgan del rio, miiiiissss hijooooossss, miiiiissss hijos…

LA LECHUZA: Esta noche voy hablar del Pirata… no puede ser! Shrrriiiieeelllll!

LA MUERTE: But the boys don't know where to find him.

EL HOMBRE SIN CABEZA: They wouldn't dream of it!

ALL: Shhh, shhhhhh. No seas tonto..cabezon!

LA LECHUZA: They could hear you and learn the secret of how to conjure El Pirata.

LA MUERTE: They mustn't dream of him. Vámonos pronto al camposanto. Bring the treasure. Hurry!! *(they exit with the chest)*

LUISITO comes out from hiding, suddenly startled again by the PIRATE who suddenly appears before him, entering swiftly, showing off his fancy swordsmanship and poise. The music score is a bright Spanish Conquistador tune.

PIRATA: *(To Luisito)* Atento, mi querido amigo. Soy, Don Escobar Maliciento Catarrunia Barcelio del Hidalgo, para servirle. But you can address me as Pirata Hidalgo! Or better yet, just Hidalgo! I am at your service. Oh, wait a minute. It is I who needs your help. Have you seen La Muerte and his infamous comrades? They are carrying my treasure!

LUISITO can't believe his eyes!

PIRATA: Espeak, muchacho, que te comieron la lengua los ratones?

LUISITO: Are you a real pirate or are you in my dreams?

PIRATE: I am both, muchacho, in flesh, alive and strong, ready to fight all that is evil, take away from the rich, give a little here, a little there, and the rest for my family that I love! But I am also a dream. I have lived many ages searching for my gold, will you help me find it? Do you know where it is?

52

LUSITO: *(aside)* This is cool! *(to the Pirate)* Yes, I know where it is. I can help you!

PIRATA: Excelente! Let's away!

LUISITO: First, you must agree to give me half of the treasure.

PIRATA: *(stops in his tracks)* Half! Pero que te han comido, los sesos los monstros? That is a very dangerous plea, my small friend.

LUISITO: But why?

PIRATA: Money for greed is evil. This is a huge quantity we are talking about. If I agree, you must have a plan.

LUSITO: Well, the boys and I only want to be filthy rich!

PIRATA: Aha! Don't be foolish, mi chico. I will agree if you help me find the treasure, but on one condición.

LUISITO: What?

PIRATA: You must promise first, on your honor, that you will be wise.

LUISITO: *(thinking)* I will.

PIRATA: Very well. Please kneel! *(Luisito obeys)* Bow your head, pequeño, and repeat after me. I... what is your name?

LUSITO: Luisisto.

PIRATA: I, Lusito, promise on my honor…

LUISITO: I, Luisito, promise on my honor…

PIRATA: …that I will search in my heart for that which I love dearly…

LUISITO: …that I will search in my heart for that which I love dearly…

PIRATA: …and for that which symbolizes my existence…

LUISITO: …and for that which symbolizes my existence…

PIRATA: …and therefore know where to share my wealth.

LUISITO: …and therefore know where to share my wealth.

PIRATA: You may stand. Te felicito, mi valiente! Now we can go, but never forget your promise and your honor. Vámonos!

LUISITO: Ok, but wait, I must bring my friends.

PIRATA: Your friends!

LUISITO: Yes, my comrades in arms! I can't go without them.

PIRATA: But I may never find you again if I lose you.

LUISITO: Oh, but trust me, I will find you.

PIRATA: Very well, I trust you are a man of honor. I will be waiting! Do not be long!

The PIRATE charges off and LUISITO is left spinning on stage, a bed is brought out where he lays down and suddenly awakes with a large grito!

LUISTO: Ama! Ama! *(to himself)* The treasure! The Pirate Hidalgo! I know what to do!

Lights out.

<u>END OF ACT ONE</u>

20/11/2

67

<u>ACT TWO</u>

SCENE 1:
CELEBRATING THANKSGIVING

RICHE and TONITA are dancing a polka in celebration of the arrival of fall. PALA, LUISITO, NUNO, ROSARIO and DALIA are clapping as LUIS enters.

PALA: Vente viejo, vamos entrándole a la polka.

RICHE: Ándale, Luis!

PALA pulls LUIS to dance with her; after a moment, LUISITO dances with DALIA, then NUNO dances with ROSARIO. All together they are dancing the fun tune. When it ends, all laugh and cheer.

As PALA speaks, ROSARIO passes out the plastic wine glasses to each adult. NUNO takes the wine bottle and pours each one some wine.

PALA: Mi familia divirtiéndose y unida es muy bueno. Yo le doy gracias a mi Tata Dios por esta nueva estación del año y del tiempo del fresco en Tejas. *(she smiles)*

LUIS: Es cierto, Pala, nuestra familia es buena y fuerte. Yo le doy gracias a Dios también porque tengo trabajo y salud. *(he flexes his muscles, and everyone laughs)*

RICHE: Y yo doy gracias pa' los caballos de mi hermano Chendo Valenzuela, especialmente al Moro de Cumpas que le ganó al Zaino de Agua Prieta, aaahoooaaaa!

Everyone agrees with a cheer!

TONITA: Yo doy gracias porque todos ustedes me aceptan así como soy… buena gente y muy platicadora.

Everyone pauses, then laughs, including TONITA.

LUIS: Y ahora Junior les va a cantar una que le enseñé. Cántala, mijo!

LUISITO: Ayy, Apa!

LUIS: Ándele mijo, aviéntate!

LUISITO centers himself as the music starts and sings "LA RAMA DEL MEZQUITE". When he finishes, all clap. (He could sing a 70's Beatles tune instead if preferred)

PALA: *(hugging Luisito)* 'Ta bueno! Ahora, todos entren a comer guajolote y papas con chile. Con mucho gusto, pasen.

They all enter, PALA at the end, but before she can enter, little MARY comes on stage with a peach pie.

MARY: Mrs. Rivera!

PALA: Mira nomas, hi, Mary what do you have there?

MARY: My daddy sent me with this peach pie my mama made for your family.

PALA: This is such a nice gift, look at you so big and so pretty. How old are you now?

MARY: Nine.

PALA: Nueve, y tan grande. Come inside 'jita, I want to give you a big plate of tamales y frijoles so you can take home with you. Entra, mi niña, entra...

Lights fade.

SCENE 2: LUISITO CONVINCES THE BOYS

NARRATOR: As you could see, the hot summer of 1976 had passed, and the fresh fall was upon the Rio Grande Valley. It was the most beautiful time of the year, and there was a certain pocket of peace in the country. The Vietnam War was over and Jimmy Carter, the peanut farmer from Georgia, had been elected president. It was the bicentennial year, and the entire Valley was hard at work. The crops were plentiful and La Pompa continued to clank and hiss, clank and hiss, as it continued its 24 hour a day heartbeat. *(pause)* But the fantasmas who had vanished for a spell were now back and determined to hide the treasure at the old Hidalgo Cemetery. A que los fantasmas…

LA MUERTE: A mí no me gustan las celebraciones. Hay mucha gente muy feliz.

EL HOMBRE SIN CABEZA: Si, y comen mucho.

LA LECHUZA: Yo estoy agradecida que no soy guajolote.

LA LLORONA: Porque mejor no nos vamos, ya mero llegamos. Síganme.

71

EL HOMBRE SIN CABEZA: Oiga, señor Don La Muerte, le puedo hacer una pregunta?

LA LECHUZA: Shriieelll, a ti nunca se te quita lo pregunton, aunque no tengas cabeza, no dejas de ser metiche.

LA MUERTE: Silencio Lechuza! Déjalo que hable.

LA LLORONA: Mejor que no diga nada porque en boca cerrada no entra mosca.

HOMBRE SIN CABEZA: Ya puedo hablar? *(they frown)* Mi pregunta es, existimos nosotros o no?

There is a long silence, and then a dog barks in the distance.

LA MUERTE: Oíste a ese perro?

EL HOMBRE SIN CABEZA nods.

LA MUERTE: Entonces para que preguntas? Vámonos!

As they make their way out across the stage, LUISITO and the BOYS approach from the opposite side.

LUISITO: Quiet, they could spot us!

JAVIER: They give me the creeps! Are you sure it's worth it?

BANDEE: Of course, it is!

JERRY: We're gonna be filthy rich! Imagine all the Mr. Q hamburgers I can eat!

NUNO: Can I buy a BB gun?

LUISITO: Quiet everyone – we're not doing it for the money.

ALL THE REST: What?

JAVIER: Have you gone crazy?

JERRY: No hamburgers?

BANDEE: I get it, Luisito wants to keep all the money for himself and he's fooling us.

LUISITO: That's not true. The Pirate changed my mind.

JANIE sneaks in nearby and hides to listen to the BOYS.

NUNO: The Hidalgo Pirate!

LUISITO: Yeah!

JAVIER: I thought you said the Pirate was from Spain.

LUISTO: He is, but his name is Hidalgo.

NUNO: What!

LUISITO: I saw him in my dream. He said he'd help us get the treasure from the fantasmas, but on one condition.

BANDEE: You saw him in a dream?

LUISITO: Yes, Tío Riche said that's how he comes to life. I'll explain later but he said we need to give the money away to something important.

BANDEE: Like what?

LUISITO: Do you remember the lady who came by the Pumphouse snoopin' around?

JAVIER: Yeah, the one who talks a lot.

JERRY: Tía Tonita talks a lot too, so what?

LUISITO: It turns out some people want to tear down La Pompa.

BANDEE: What?

NUNO: Nobody can tear down La Pompa, it's been here forever!

LUISITO: That's right, and that's what we're gonna do with the money: we're gonna save La Pompa.

JERRY: What money?

JAVIER: The treasure, tonto!

JERRY: Oh, yeah!

BANDEE: So, what's this lady got to do with all of it?

LUISTO: She's a historian and thinks La Pompa should be a museum.

NUNO: What's a museum?

JAVIER: A place where they have dinosaur bones, loco.

JERRY: Whoa! Where will the dinosaur bones come from?

LUISITO: No dummy, a museum is a place where you preserve history and art.

BANDEE: Will this keep the Pumphouse from being torn down?

LUISITO: I think so, that's why we got to get that money, to help preserve the Pumphouse.

NUNO: Can we still go swimming?

The BOYS give him an incredulous stare.

JAVIER: I'm in, how about you guys?

The BOYS all agree.

LUISITO: But we're also gonna have to join the girls with their report on the history of the Pumphouse.

JERRY: No way, Luisito! You just want to hang around Janie 'cause you like her!

NUNO: Yeah, Luisito, she always calls you over for Red Rover Red Rover!

LUISITO: Nombre, you guys don't get it, we have to contribute to the report to prove to the historian lady that we don't want the Pumphouse to disappear, and with the money from the treasure it could be turned into a museum forever.

The BOYS are too confused to make this out.

LUSITO: You have to trust me, it'll work.

JERRY: Can we at least have a little money for hamburgers and fries and cokes... maybe?

They all look at LUISITO as though their agreement depends on his answer.

LUISITO: Ok!

They all cheer and high five and make silly sounds.

LUISITO: Now all I have to do is dream.

JAVIER: What?

LUISITO: Dream the Pirate! Come on, you guys, let's make a plan.

ALL TOGETHER: Let's save the Pumphouse... La Pompa, La Pompa, La Pompa, La Pompa!

The BOYS run off and JANIE comes on stage from hiding on the boys. ORALIA appears and scares her.

JANIE: Oralia!

ORALIA: Que pasa, calabaza?

JANIE: We have to save La Pompa.

ORALIA: La Pompa?

JANIE: You heard right, let's go!

They both run off. Lights fade.

SCENE 3: EL ROSARIO

PALA and TONITA are sitting with veils over their head, holding rosaries, praying.

PALA: Ayy, comadre, los fantasmas todavía andan sueltos.

TONITA: Dicen que La Llorona le salió a mi hermano Juan.

PALA: El Diablo siempre anda suelto. A nosotros nos salió el otro día, y se quería llevar a Luisito.

TONITA: Ayyy, Maria Purísima! Me da miedo al pensarlo.

PALA: Por eso es bueno rezar y pedirle a nuestro Dios que nos ayude siempre.

An unexpected loud knock is heard at the door. The WOMEN let out a scream.

RICHE: *(offstage)* Soy yo, Riche, puedo entrar?

PALA: Pasa, hombre, que me diste un susto, pensé que eras El Diablo!

TONITA: Que quieres, Riche?

RICHE: Disculpen que las molesto, pero quería pedirles unos rezos para los caballos de mi hermano Chendo. Ya va a retirar el Moro y el Alazán y necesito un corral para cuidarlos del matadero. Son tan bonitos animales, es una lástima que se pierdan.

PALA: 'Ta bueno, Riche, we'll pray for your horses. By the way, did you see Doña Jovita and Esperanza on your way here?

RITCHE: Oh sí, pero como es el día del tricky tricky, ese Halloween mentado, pues no las conocía como andan tantas brujas y fantasmas allá afuera, pues las confundí. Bueno, ya me voy, hay les encargo los rezos.

TONITA: Que tricky tricky que ni tus patas, viejo sin vergüenza! Anda, déjanos solas y cuidado que no te vaya pasar la lechuza y te hecha la cosa blanca, si así ya te dan unos temblorones para que quieres más. *(he yells boo at them and leaves)* Se me hace que esas viejas no vienen, Pala. Mejor le seguimos solas al rosario.

BOTH: Dios te salve, Maria, llena eres de gracia, el Señor es contigo. Bendita eres entre todas las mujeres, y bendito es el fruto de tu vientre, Jesús. Santa Maria, Madre de Dios, ruega por nosotros, pecadores, ahora y en la hora de nuestra muerte. Amen.

As the faithful WOMEN pray, a baby is heard crying in the distance followed by the wind and the cries of LA LLORONA. Unseen by the women, LA LLORONA crosses the stage behind them with extended arms. The WOMEN are frightened.

TONITA: Ayy, Pala, vámonos pa' la cocina donde hay más luz.

PALA: Sí, vamos.

LA MUERTE appears from the other side of the stage and laughs. The WOMEN turn and see him with LA LLORONA. They scream and run out.

LA MUERTE: Esta gente se asusta con la nada.

LA LLORONA: No te creas, si debes verte en el espejo un día de estos.

He turns to look at her and offers a sarcastic laugh. Lights fade.

SCENE 4: MRS. STONEWALL DROPS BY

RUFUS and LUIS once again are working at the Pumphouse with the oil can and the hammer. They are both in a very cheerful mood.

RUFUS: Did you pass out any candies to the kids last night?

LUIS: I sure did. Pala and her friends were praying the rosary when I asked my primo Lucio and Alma to go in and scare them; they were dressed like La Muerte and La Llorona. Man, they looked like the real thing – it's good I was drinking a few cervezas. How about you?

RUFUS: Not too many kids come back to the house, but my kids went out and brought back tons a candy. *(beat)* I swear I thought I saw La Llorona y La Muerte – maybe it was your cousin.

A car door is slammed.

LUIS: Here comes that nice lady again, what's her name?

RUFUS: Mrs. Stonewall.

LUIS: Ah, Pared de Piedra.

MRS STONEWALL: Gentleman, I see you're both hard at work, so I won't take much of your time, but I was wondering, could I ask you a few more questions about the Pumphouse?

RUFUS: Sure.

MRS. STONEWALL: Thank you very much. So how important do you think this place is?

Both MEN look at each other.

RUFUS: The Pumphouse irrigates farms in Alamo, San Juan, and Pharr, over 70,000 acres of land that needs water all the time. Sometimes the engines wear down, but the farmers don't understand that – they just want water all the time. *(he chuckles)* These engines need 24 hour-a-day supervision, and it's my job to keep them running well. Of course, we work 12-hour days, sometimes even 14 and 16 hours to make sure these engines and pumps work properly. Otherwise, I can't complain about anything.

MRS STONEWALL: How have things changed over the years?

RUFUS: When I first started, I made $20 a week. I could buy three bags of groceries and have money left. Of course, I get paid more today. I have fourteen kids, and my Margaret is the best wife in the world, and that hasn't changed. *(he chuckles)*

MRS STONEWALL: Is the work difficult or dangerous?

RUFUS: Oh, it gets real hot in there, especially in the summertime, it makes things miserable. Once we had a boy who got sick on us, he was so hot he went kind of haywire: he imagined the boiler was on fire. One day I found him passed out lying between two engines he was oiling down in the pits. When I spotted him, he had his arm stretched out with his oil cup asking me, with a faint murmur, to continue oiling the engines to keep them from burning their barrens. He was a dedicated worker, but after that he got sick and quit working with us. *(pause)*

MRS STONEWALL: Oh, that poor man! But aside from operating these giant machines and the difficult times, have there been any fond memories?

Both RUFUS and LUIS smile.

RUFUS: Well, just last week I saw Johnny Franz catch a fish with his little boy John David. A month ago, I saw Luis save his boy from drowning. I saved my son Joe too. Let's see, oh yeah, we saw the Headless Man, La Lechuza and the Weeping Woman, a hurricane nearly wiped us out, the boys started diving off the Pumphouse shed nearly 40 feet tall – that was exciting! – and we never get tired of eating fresh catfish.

MRS STONEWALL: Imagine all that!

RUFUS: Oh, yeah! *(getting excited)* I made a net out of chicken wire to catch fish. One time a boy who used to work for me caught 42 catfish at the same time. He yelled out, "Come on and help me with these fish, Rufus!" Boy, was that a mighty fine catch, big ones and small ones, all of 'em catfish.

The three share a laugh.

MRS STONEWALL: So, for all these years since the early 1900's, water has been pumped non-stop?

RUFUS: Only when the big rains come do, we slow down, but we still pump for the city drinking water and for washing.

LUIS: I hope you can preserve this place so others can come and appreciate what was done here and to learn how the engines and boilers operated.

MRS. STONEWALL: I'm sure going to try. I hope I can help raise the funds, when the time comes, together with the city of Hidalgo and others who are interested in keeping this place alive, maybe even turn it into a museum.

LUIS: Is this place going out of business anytime soon?

MRS. STONEWALL: Well, the future changes things, what with innovative machinery and greater efficiency. One day the pumps will all be electric and will have to be moved down river to catch the natural flow of water. Unfortunately, when that happens, this place will stop operating.

LUIS: *(astonished)* That's unbelievable! Where will the boys go swimming? *(sentimental)* I'm gonna miss this place, el Corazón de Hidalgo, La Pompa.

MRS STONEWALL: Oh, Mr. Rivera, try not to get so emotional! I'm going to work hard to save the Pumphouse. *(beat)* Now, Mr. Wisdom, you mentioned something a minute ago about a weeping woman and a headless man?

LUIS: Don't forget La Lechuza y La Muerte too.

MRS STONEWALL: *(hesitates over the Spanish words)* *La* Lechooza and La Mooairtay. Who are they?

RUFUS: La Muerte is death and La Lechuza is the big white owl that spits the white stuff on you to make you shake.

MRS STONEWALL *(writing this down)* A white owl, Death, a headless man and a weeping woman? Are you serious?

LUIS: Yes, ma'am, these are the boogeyman of the Rio Grande valley. *(LUIS and RUFUS nod and share a wide smile. Mrs. STONEWALL is amused)*

MRS STONEWALL: Well, this sure adds another dimension to the story! Do all the folks around here believe in these fantasy creatures? *(she's smiling)*

LUIS and RUFUS begin a slow retreat backwards as the FANTASMAS appear behind MRS. STONEWALL pulling their treasure chest.

LUIS: Well, don't look now Mrs. Stonewall, but it looks like los fantasmas heard you!

The FANTASMAS stop and face MRS. STONEWALL. LUIS and RUFUS run off stage. The FANTASMAS start their sounds, MRS. STONEWALL turns to look, the FANTASMAS become louder, and she screams and runs for her life. Lights out.

SCENE 5: ANCIENT HISTORY

JANIE and the GIRLS including ORALIA are practicing the dance again. It's a water dance from the Aztec-Mayan cultures with drums and flutes and props and costumes and movements

ORALIA: Can we take a break now?

JANIE: Ok, chavalonas, let's take a break.

DALIA: This dance is exhausting, but I like it!

MARY: Where did it come from?

ROSARIO: The ancient culture. The dance has to be powerful like the Rio Grande.

JANIE: Nothing less! *(beat)* Ok, more on our written report, listen to this. Hidalgo used to be called La Habitación.

MARY: What does *that* mean?

ORALIA: It means a place to stay.

DALIA: Who named it?

JANIE: The early Spanish settlers led by Jose de Escandón in 1749. Then a ferry was built for crossing the river and later the town became known as Edinburgh with an H and finally Hidalgo in 1876, named after el Padre Miguel Hidalgo, the liberator of Mexico.

ROSARIO: Indians lived here way before the Spaniards, nomadic tribes referred to as Coahuiltecans. The Karankawas and Carrizos lived closer to the Gulf Coast.

MARY: What happened to them?

ROSARIO: I haven't gotten that far with my research, but I'll let you know.

DALIA: I want to know.

ORALIA: Me too. *(beat)* Oh, and my father said that the city of Pharr is also very instrumental in the valley's agricultural success. Pharr has nearly 23 fruit and vegetable packing and shipping companies that serve farmers and the agriculture business. Pharr's a big city now!

JANIE: Awesome, lets include the city of Pharr's contributions in our report!

LUISITO and the BOYS enter on their way to the canal.

ORALIA: Here comes trouble! Hey, Luisito, where are you guys going?

NUNO: Don't tell her.

JERRY: So, you girls really think you're smarter than us?

MARY: What's this about?

JAVIER: We know all about your book report on the Pumphouse…

BANDEE: Did you know it was in trouble?

LUISITO: No, it's not. *(elbows BANDEE)* Come on you guys, let's move on.

JANIE: Wait a minute, if the Pumphouse is in trouble, we can help.

LUISITO: Suppose it *was* in trouble, how could you help?

JANIE: We can help you dream up the Pirate.

NUNO: What Pirate?

JAVIER: Yeah, what Pirate?

LUISITO: How do you know about him?

JANIE: 'Cuz I saw you with him.

MARY: What Pirate?

JANIE: The one who will help Luisito get the treasure from the fantasmas.

ROSARIO: What treasure?

LUISITO: Janie, I think you and I should talk about this in private.

The GIRLS do the shane, shane, shane thing again.

JANIE & LUISITO: Cut it out, this is serious.

BANDEE: Yeah, the survival of the Pumphouse may depend on us and the treasure.

DALIA: Ok, but there's no way the rest of us are leaving, we want to hear the details and be involved.

JANIE: Fine, this is what we'll do. Us girls will continue researching the Pumphouse and present the best history report of all.

DALIA: And our dance just gets better all the time.

JANIE: Great, then after our school presentation, we'll have a public performance at the Pumphouse compuertas, and we'll invite the whole town and the historian lady from Washington... what's her name?

NUNO: Mrs. Stonewall. *(everybody looks at him astonished he knew her name)* I heard mi Apá talk about her, but he calls her Pared de Piedra.

DALIA: I get it, this will help everyone know that our Pumphouse is special.

JANIE: That's it!

LUISITO: Ok, and what do *we* do?

JANIE: You boys have to get the treasure and keep your promise to the Pirate.

LUISITO: You know about the condition?

JANIE: Yeah, I heard it all. Anyway, the money from the treasure will help the Pumphouse become a museum when it shuts down. *(beat)* I saw the Pirate... like a dream. He's so brave, like you, Luisito… *(the girls are about to do another shane, shane, shane but are quickly stopped by a stern stare from Janie and all the boys) I* know the two of you together will defeat los fantasmas.

LUISITO: Yeah, he is awesome. *(beat)* But after we get the money, how are we gonna get it into the right hands, to Mrs. Stonewall? After all, we're just kids and she'd never believe where it came from.

MARY: I have an idea! We can arrange an anonymous donation to a trust account in the name of the Hidalgo Pumphouse Preservation Fund. The money is so old no one will claim it. We just need to find an adult we can trust to set it up for us.

Everyone is silent for a long moment; they can't believe so much intelligence from this kid.

MARY: Did I ever tell you my uncle, who now lives with us, used to be a banker from Kansas City?

EVERYONE: Oooooohhhhhhh!

ROSARIO: I told you girls are smarter than boys.

DALIA: If this will help save La Pompa, then I'm in.

Everyone is energized, determined.

ORALIA: I'm gonna practice the dance till my heart beats as loud as the Pumphouse.

JERRY: Once I ate three hamburgers in one day.

89

NUNO: When I grow up, I want to be an astronaut.

EVERYONE: What?

NUNO just shrugs his shoulders.

BANDEE: I wanna be a scientist to study the female brain!

JAVIER: I'm gonna swim the entire length of the Rio Grande from Southern Colorado to Boca Chica, Brownsville!

JANIE: I'm gonna be in the Miss America pageant!

JAVIER: I want to be a filmmaker and make a movie about a famous pirate who finds his true love! *(he smiles at Janie)*

EVERYONE: *(the others catch on) Shane*, shane, shane! Lusito loves Janie, Luisito loves Janie! Shane, shane, shane!

Big bright music comes up as the KIDS playfully chase each other on stage. After a moment, the music ends and they all shout:

EVERYONE: Let's away!

Lights out.

SCENE 6: LA TORTILLA Y LA CARA DE CRISTO

LUIS is sitting on the chair reading the paper. PALA is standing nearby.

PALA: Ayy mi Luis, I'm so glad you have this Sunday off to spend some time with me. I'm preparing you una carnita guisada con gravy y unas tortillitas bien sabrosas.

LUIS: *(reading his newspaper not paying much attention)* 'Ta bueno, Pala.

PALA: Guess what Luisito was doing today?

LUIS: What?

PALA: He was plucking feathers from our geese and ducks, dice to make a good pillow because he wants to sleep well so he can dream, these kids nowadays have many ideas, viejo.

LUIS: Yeah.

PALA: *(beat)* Someone told me a pretty woman stopped by the Pumphouse, Luis, do you know her? *(he doesn't hear her)* Te estoy hablando.

LUIS: What?

PALA: La mujer at the Pumphouse, what does she want?

LUIS: She's a historian.

PALA: A historian, what's that?

LUIS: A person who studies and archives history.

PALA: Is she studying you?

LUIS: She wants to save the Pumphouse.

PALA: Save the Pumphouse? From what? It's made of brick and metal; nothing is going to happen to it.

LUIS: If it closes down one day, she wants it to be a museum, that's all. *(he smells something from the kitchen)* What's burning?

PALA: Mis tortillas, ayy Luis!

PALA runs out. LUIS continues to read.

PALA: *(offstage)* Luis! Luis! Ven pronto, ven!

He doesn't move. She returns holding a tortilla in her palm.

PALA: Qué ves aquí, mira bien, que miras?

She practically places the tortilla before his face. He finally looks up and sees it.

LUIS: *(surprised)* Es el rostro de Cristo Jesús, the face of Jesus!

PALA: Sí Luis, es un milagro de nuestro Señor… es un milagro! *(he stands and they freeze)*

NARRATOR: As the two stood there in their small wooden house observing the miracle, the rooster crowed and the mountain moved. The children slept peaceful tucked in warm goose feather blankets and soft rabbit furs. Luisito dreamed of the Pirate. Rufus and Margaret held hands on the porch as the colorful butterflies landed on fragrant flowers and leaves. The river was calm, and the evil spirits were nowhere in sight. Riche listened to a Detroit Tigers Baseball game on his tiny transistor radio and Tonita prayed the rosary. The miracle of la tortilla was a blessing. La vida would continue in the small town and everything would get better.

PALA: Dios nos protege y nada malo nunca nos podrá afectar.

LUIS: Eres una buena mujer, Pala, positiva, una buena esposa, que Dios me regaló.

PALA: Y tú, mi Luis, un querido esposo, fuerte, que el cielo me ha entregado.

They embrace gently as the lights fade. Lights out.

SCENE 7: THE BOYS BATTLE LOS FANTASMAS

LUISITO is sleeping comfortably on the bed when suddenly a misty enchanting music is heard, and the lights slowly become brighter. LUISITO turns over as the PIRATE appears and takes center stage. He is fencing with an imaginary foe. LUISITO sits up.

PIRATA: I am here, young master of the sea. Your dream is a reality. Arise from thy slumber to face the dreaded task, to fight away the evil spirits who cannot overcome the goodness in us. Arriba, pequeño, que ya está aquí tu Hidalgo, y el tesoro nos espera!

LUISITO rises ready to join EL PIRATA, as LA LECHUZA flies by making her loud shrill cry.

LUISITO: Hidalgo, it's good to see you again, it's time.

PIRATA: Over 200 years have passed since I've seen my beloved, but this day my heart will rejoice. Once we defeat the fantasmas and regain the treasure then I shall return to her... *(imagining with lovely delight)* Come, chico, the time is now!

The BOYS appear one by one with wooden swords and one for LUISITO as well.

ALL OF THEM: We are here! *(JERRY tosses a sword to LUISITO)*

LUISITO: Then what are we waiting for? Lead the way, Hidalgo!

They exit and the FANTASMAS enter, except for LA LECHUZA, who appears moments later. They enter el camposanto de Hidalgo where unmarked tombstones abound.

EL HOMBRE SIN CABEZA: Over here, I think I see the perfect spot to hide el tesoro!

LA LLORONA: Pero tú no puedes ver, no tienes cabeza.

EL HOMBRE SIN CABEZA: Eso crees tú, I can see with my soul. *(breaking down)* I was a living man once. I had a head. I knew about love. I had my chance. I…

LA MUERTE: Está bien, ya déjense de tonterías, el amor no existe… miren, allí viene La Lechuza!

LA LECHUZA makes her shrill cry and flies in.

LA LECHUZA: Hurry, let's hide the treasure, we are being pursued.

LA MUERTE: Quién nos busca?

LA LECHUZA: Es el Pirata Hidalgo and his recruits!

They all let out a yell of despair.

LA LLORONA: *(nostalgic)* Mi hombre fue así como el Pirata, mi mancebo ilustre y de hermoso talla, en sus brazos me durmió… (*she becomes upset*) Así fue el que me engañó… Ayy, mis hijos… ayy, mis hijos… vénganse…

LA MUERTE: Cállense zarampahuilos! Vamos a enterrar el tesoro en esa tumba que no tiene nombre *(pointing to an unmarked grave stone)* para que todos la olviden y solo nosotros la encontremos. Pronto escarba, descabezado inútil.

EL HOMBRE SIN CABEZA: Porqué me insultas, huesuda infraganti?! Yo te enseñaré a respetar… defiéndete!

The PIRATE and the BOYS rush in, the FANTASMAS turn their attention to them, thus beginning a huge battle. The lights flicker, thunder is heard, and the music is brilliant. The HEADLESS MAN refuses to fight and stands back, wildly strumming his flamenco guitar. Suddenly PALA and JANIE appear with buckets of holy water which they throw onto the fighting spirits, who all yell:

FANTASMAS: Agua bendita! Agua bendita! Holy water! Nooooooo!

The FANTASMAS begin to back away, except for the HEADLESS MAN who has distanced himself. The treasure remains center stage. The FANTASMAS are retreating in defeat.

LA MUERTE: Esto no termina, Piratita. Ya volveremos por más almas y más riquezas... ya volveremos... *(to the HEADLESS MAN)* Y tú que ni para usar un sombrero sirves, siempre fuiste traidor. Vámonos!

NUNO: Tengo miedo y quiero a mi ama!

EVERYONE: Sshhh! Sea hombre, Nuno!

NUNO runs over to the arms of his mother PALA.

LUISITO: Mama, Janie, how did you know we were here?

PALA: Pues sabrá Dios, mijo, todo parece un sueño. Pero vale más que no te andes yendo pa' el canal. Y ustedes que hacen allí parados. Y tú, señor Pirata, ya Halloween pasó. Vámonos pa' la casa, todos, vénganse.

PALA exits with NUNO and JANIE.

PIRATA: *(clearing his throat)* What is Halloween? *(beat)* A job well done, my comrades! What matters is not how the task was completed but that goodness has prevailed, that is what is meant by honor. *(he sees the boys are not buying it)* Honor thy father, honor thy mother, *(sigh)* and thy love, *(deep sigh, looking into the heavens with a hand on the heart),* oh, thy love. I, Hidalgo, el Dorado, will never change. I am love and respect for those who yearn for sympathy, courage, and strength to take another step forward in their struggles, to survive against the harsh storms of life. *(beat)* Today I will reunite with my true love and I will share my wealth. I will uplift my people who depend on me. *(to Luisito)* You, my pequeño, know what you must do. *(beat)* Chamacos! Que viva Hidalgo! *(they repeat "Que viva!")* Que viva Pharr! *(they repeat "Que viva!")* y que viva La Pompa y El Rio Grande! *(they repeat "Que viva!")* The treasure is yours, Luisito. Mine I take in my heart and in my soul. Save your beloved Pumphouse, the greatest memory of your juventud. Save La Pompa... and mankind shall never forget you. *(beat)* I must away!

LUISITO: Gracias, Hidalgo, el Dorado, the golden one, you have opened our eyes. We will never be the same.

JAVIER: Comrades, let's hear three cheers for Hidalgo!

ALL TOGETHER: Hip hip hooray! Hip hip hooray! Hip hip hooray! Long live Hidalgo!

HIDALGO takes a bow. His entrance music is heard as he fences his way off stage. We hear his voice as though faraway and getting farther.

PIRATA *(offstage)* Live long, my friends… live wise… and be loved.

THE BOYS: Whoa!

JANIE runs back in.

JANIE: Luisito, the treasure! We must get it into the trust fund, but how?

RICHE enters arguing with TONITA, not noticing the BOYS.

RICHE: All I ever wanted was to care for old beat down horses!

TONITA: But you need money to buy the sheriff's corral, where will you get it?

RICHE: I will find it; my prayers will be answered, mujer!

TONITA: Ayy, hombre, eres más terco que una mula! *(she exits)*

RICHE: *(yelling)* Taking care of old horses is a good thing, mujer! You should know!

EVERYONE: Don Riche! He'll be our donor!

RICHE: *(startled, he yells) Ayy*, muchachos, pero que están haciendo aquí? Ya mero me daban un heart attack. (*more fun karate moves*) I could've killed you!

The kids cluster around him lovingly and embrace him.
They pick up the treasure chest and carry it off with Don
Riche as they raise his spirit.

NARRATOR: Don Riche was quite a character. Once he
had gone all the way to Detroit, Michigan, to work on
automobiles at the Great Lakes Steel Mill factory, but after
one winter he came back to the Valley saying he'd almost
froze to death and that he's much rather work on horses and
in the onion fields. He wasn't very educated, but he sure
knew about a lot of things. It seemed as though good luck
always accompanied him. His life was about to change
once again.

SCENE 8: INCREDULOUS

RUFUS and LUIS are talking down right stage by the
compuertas.

RUFUS: Hey Luis, I saw your brother-in-law. He was
walking six old horses on the levee to the sheriff's corral,
singing all the way. I heard he bought the place. How you
figure he did that?

LUIS: I don't know, Rufus, but he said he came across an
inheritance by a long-lost relative from old Spain.

RUFUS: Spain?

LUIS: That's what he said. He claims his great-great-great
uncle was a pirate.

RUFUS: Was that two greats or three?

LUIS: Uh, *(counts on fingers)* three.

RUFUS: You don't say.

LUIS: I think it's all the stories he's heard from Tonita. That woman can sure whip 'em up.

They freeze. Lights out on them and lights up on TONITA and PALA. Both WOMEN are standing up right center stage.

TONITA: Oye, Pala, no sé dónde sacó Riche tanto dinero pero dice que de hoy en adelante solo va cuidar caballos. Tú, que sabes?

PALA: Pues no sé, pero los huercos dicen que ya no han visto pasar La Lechuza.

TONITA: Quién 'ta hablando de La Lechuza, mujer?

PALA: Ayy Tonita, no te ensalces. *(beat)* Que bueno que dejaste de decirles tantos cuentos a los huercos porque ya me la creía yo también.

TONITA: Desde que te salió la tortilla con nuestro Señor no habido cuento más grande.

PALA: Ha venido mucha gente a rezar con la tortilla y a pedir milagros. También la Pared de Piedra vino.

TONITA: Adio!

PALA: Quiere un milagro para que no tumben La Pompa.

TONITA: Padre Santo, fíjate nomas!

PALA: Y los huercos ya presentaron su historia en la escuela, y ahora lo van a pasar también en La Pompa.

TONITA: Pues Dios es muy grande y todo va a salir bien. Pero quien sabe de dónde sacó tanto dinero Riche?

PALA: Vámonos pa' La Pompa, vente!

Lights out on them. They exit. Lights up on RUFUS and LUIS.

RUFUS: Why do you suppose we haven't heard los fantasmas or smelled any bad odors lately?

LUIS: I think it's because I changed my deodorant. *(he laughs)*

RUFUS: Come again?

LUIS: The fantasmas stopped appearing ever since my wife's tortilla came out.

RUFUS: That's right. *(beat)* Hey, I almost forgot we gotta get to the Pumphouse for the kids. Mrs. Stonewall said she'd be there too, vamos!

Lights out on them. They exit.

SCENE 9: JANIE'S SONG

LUISITO appears from left stage. JANIE from the right.

JANIE: Luisito! Wait up, aren't you going to La Pompa?

LUISITO: I'm going for the boys.

JANIE: What we did for the Pumphouse was really cool, think anyone will ever believe it?

LUISITO: No.

JANIE: It was like a dream.

LUISITO: It *was* a dream. It's just funny how we were all a part of it.

JANIE: It's because we love the same things. *(pause)* Older people call it youthful innocence.

LUISITO: I guess you're right.

JANIE: I hope we can always be friends.

He nods.

JANIE: *(beat)* It sure was fun preparing Don Riche for his big appointment at the Border Bank. He kept saying, *(mimicking DON RICHE)* "Two million dollars is enough for 10 lifetimes!" (t*hey laugh*)

LUIS: I can't wait to see the expression on Mrs. Stonewall's face. *(beat)* I'll get the boys and meet you at the pump. (*he starts off*)

JANIE: Wait a minute! Since there won't be time to sing my song at the Pumphouse today, would you like to hear it?

LUISITO: Sure.

The music starts and JANIE asks LUISITO to sit on the stairs. She sings "CRUZARÉ LA MONTAÑA" by Selena Quintanilla.

JANIE: Did you like it?

LUISITO: *(tender)* It's the most beautiful song I've ever heard.

JANIE: *(pause)* I love you, Luisito. You always know what to say. (*she smiles*)

He smiles back and after a pondering moment she says:

JANIE: Let's go!

Both exit separate ways. Light change.

SCENE 10: THE PUMPHOUSE IS SAVED

DON RICHE enters from up right stage to center stage wearing a fine suit. He addresses the audience:

RICHE: Well, come on everybody, this is going to be one BIG celebration!

Big happy music begins, like from Zoo suit, maybe a swing number. RUFUS, TONITA, PALA and LUIS enter all dressed up. They string a banner that says "LONG LIVE LA POMPA & THE RIO GRANDE" across the backstage wall. The BOYS arrive and help set up the stage for the speeches and the final dance. RUFUS places himself in the center to address the audience and the music fades.

RUFUS: Can I have your attention, please? Can I have your attention? Thank you. As you all know, I'm Rufus Wisdom. I really don't like speaking in public very much, but I do have to say that I'm proud of the kids for speaking mighty fine about our Pumphouse, and about all we do here for the Valley's agriculture. *(pause) And* now, my work partner Luis Rivera will say a word or two.

LUIS: Pues, yo quería decir lo mismo que dijo Rufus. Estos niños son lo más bonito en la vida. Me hacen recordar a mi tata que quise mucho y que me enseño a trabajar aquí en La Pompa… oooooooooooooooo hace muuuuuuuchos años. *(everyone laughs)* I hope this place can be a museum one day for education and folklore.

LUIS becomes sentimental when offstage we hear screams and MRS. STONEWALL runs in.

MRS. STONEWALL: *(shouting)* A miracle, everyone a miracle! Un milagro!

ALL: Allí viene la Stonewall!

MRS STONEWALL: Sorry I'm a bit late, but I could not believe my ears! I just got off the phone with the Smithsonian board of directors, and they informed me that a mysterious bank account for 1 and ¾ million dollars has appeared in the name of the Hidalgo Pumphouse Preservation Trust Fund, to save La Pompa!

LUIS: Does this mean it will become a museum?

MRS. STONEWALL: Oh, it sure looks that way! *(crosses to PALA)* Es un milagro, Pala. That tortilla really does work! *(EVERYONE laughs)*

PALA: *(embracing MRS. STONEWALL)* Ahh que, Mrs. Stonewall, when I first heard about you, I thought you wanted to research my Luis. *(she chuckles)* But now I see what a great woman you are. All this work you did to preserve our history. We all owe you a great debt. *(beat)* And now, our girls have prepared the final part of their history report with a dance in honor of our beautiful Rio Grande that provides us with life on behalf of our creator. Entren, mijitas!

The ancient music begins as the GIRLS position themselves and dance honorably and gracefully in beautiful Aztec garb and head dress. They finish with much peace as the lights slowly fade to black. ALL exit.

THE END

EXTRA ENDING SCENE: (OPTIONAL)

This scene features the original song, LA POMPA DE HIDALGO written and arranged by Wally Gonzalez, The Short-legged Texan.

After the last scene of the play and the blackout the lights come back instead of the curtain call the FANTASMAS appear on stage. They are much calmer, almost realistic.

LA MUERTE: Me duele admitirlo, pero me gusto el cuento.

LA LLORONA: Ayy, mi muertito, que cosas dices.

EL HOMBRE SIN CABEZA: Ya escucharon la nueva canción?

LA LECHUZA: I heard Wally Gonzalez, the short-Legged Texan, from 26 1/2 street in McAllen who once sang a song about El Pajaro Grande, wrote a new song for La Pompa.

ALL OF THEM: Que que?

EL HOMBRE SIN CABEZA: Wasn't that about El Walmart?

LA LLORONA: No, that was another one, but this one is about La Pompa, óiganla, aquí les va!

The Wally Gonzalez song is played and the FANTASMAS dance. When it ends, the lights fade and they slowly y exit as the lights come down.

Acknowledgement: The authors Lucio G Rivera and Pedro Garcia also wish to thank Mr. Wally Gonzalez, music extraordinaire, for writing and arranging the fun song, La Pompa De Hidalgo, exclusively for our premier of the play in 2011. It's a comical catchy cumbia with a bit of rap in Spanish. Here are the lyrics to the song:

106

LA POMPA DE HIDALGO
written and performed by Wally Gonzalez aka The Short-Legged Texan.

La pompa de Hidalgo, la pompa de Hidalgo
es historia del valle del Rio Grande

La pompa de Hidalgo, la pompa de Hidalgo
es leyenda del valle del Rio Grande
(rap)

Nació en 1909 hasta 1983
y muy asombrados se van a quedar
porque tiene el equipo original

van a ver una escuela muy vieja donde sale la llorona y se
queja..
se aparece un hombre sin cabeza
según dicen es el tío de Teresa

(chorus)

La pompa de Hidalgo, la pompa de Hidalgo
es historia en el valle de Rio Grande

La pompa de Hidalgo, la pompa de Hidalgo
es leyenda del valle de Rio Grande

repeat

Special Edition I

Once Upon a Time Around the Hidalgo Pumphouse

(The Adventures of the Boys and Fantasmas)
Written by Lucio G.Rivera

The Hidalgo Pumphouse is located next to the Rio Grande River in South Texas. In 1933, a major hurricane changed the course of the river to its current location.

The pump house was built in 1909, but its story begins around 1886. The river brought water to thousands of acres of crops, and landowners depended completely on the Hidalgo Pumphouse and the Rio Grande River for their crops to flourish.

The canal was a favorite swimming and fishing spot for the local youngsters and their elders who lived in the City of Hidalgo (see enclosed photo of swimming area around pump house). In fact, it was the early settlers and landowners who were so very influential in the growth of Hidalgo County and the city itself. They built and operated the early shops of the town, and many of those same folks worked at the pump house. Some of the families are listed below. This is their story.

Rufus Wisdom Family: Pump house Supervisor

Fedrico Rodriguez and his wife. Lolita Resendez: Humble Gas Station – (6 children)

Benino Alonzo and his wife, Lolita: Grocery Store - (son,

Mamiliano Alonzo, a.k.a. "Marni")

Bartolo Rivera and his wife, Irene Rocha: Pumphouse Worker - (12 children)

Luis Rivera and his wife, Pabla, a.k.a. "Pala": Pump house Worker for 60 years.

The late Pedro "La Pirucha" Garcia and family.

Bartolo Rivera: Helped build the Hidalgo Pumphouse where he worked with other Anglo supervisors. He trained his son, Luis, to keep the furnaces burning to create enough steam for the huge engines to propel the Rio Grande water into the canals to irrigate the various crops on the United States side of the river; sugar cane, tomatoes, carrots, cabbage, cauliflower, chili peppers, onions, cotton, and watermelon depended on this water source.

Today the Hidalgo Pump house continues to bring life and vitality to the region. The pump house, now serving as a historical museum, is a center for history and culture for the Rio Grande Valley; and the sounds of running water can still be heard in the distance coming through the *compuertas* of *el canal*. And paying tribute to the past memories; to all those individuals and organizations dedicated in keeping the preservation of old Hidalgo's buildings and its history.

[Swimming area around old pump house]

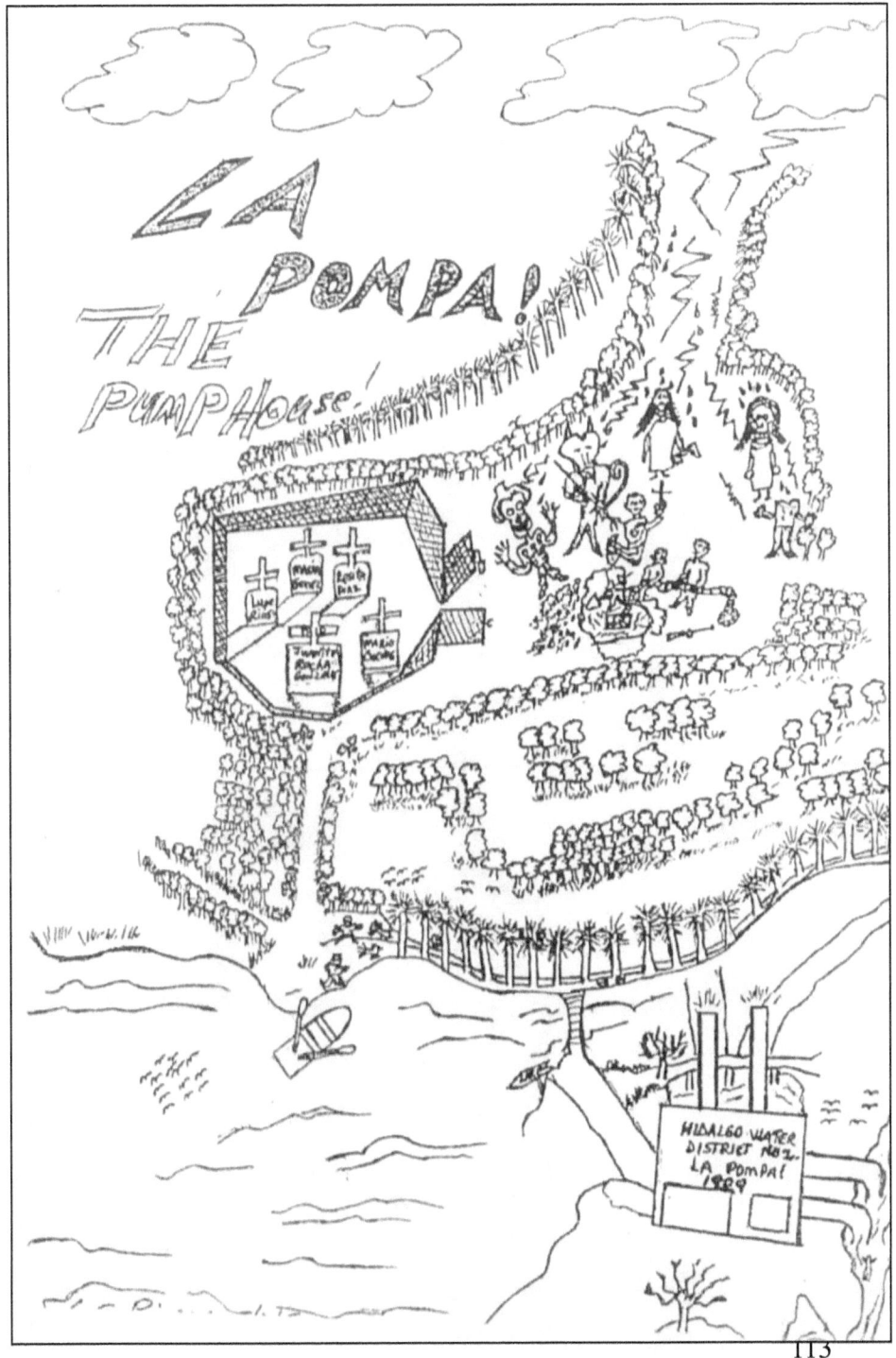

La Muerte: Also known as the skullman, *La Muerte*
    is part of the *Fantasmas*.

He closely guards the treasure.

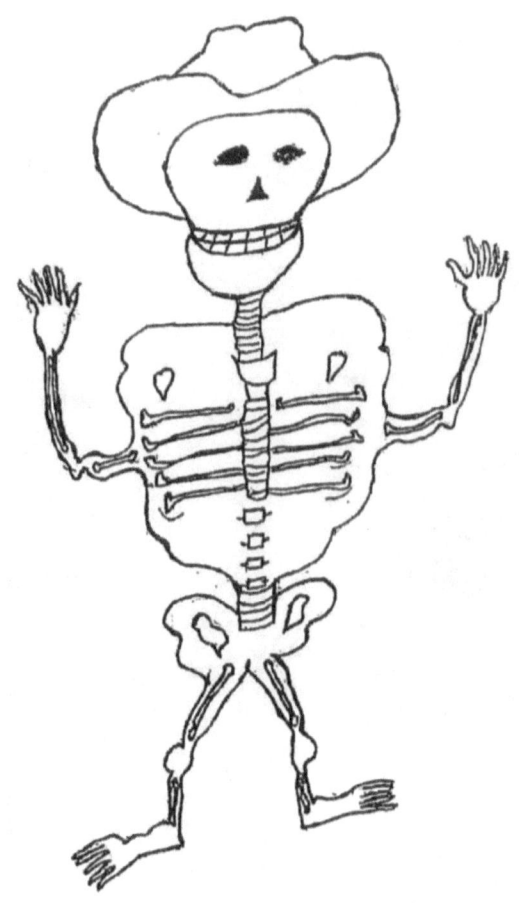

LA MUERTE

El Creature. Also known as *El Cucoo*, he is wicked
and does evil things.

He has control of the *Fantasmas* and the treasure.

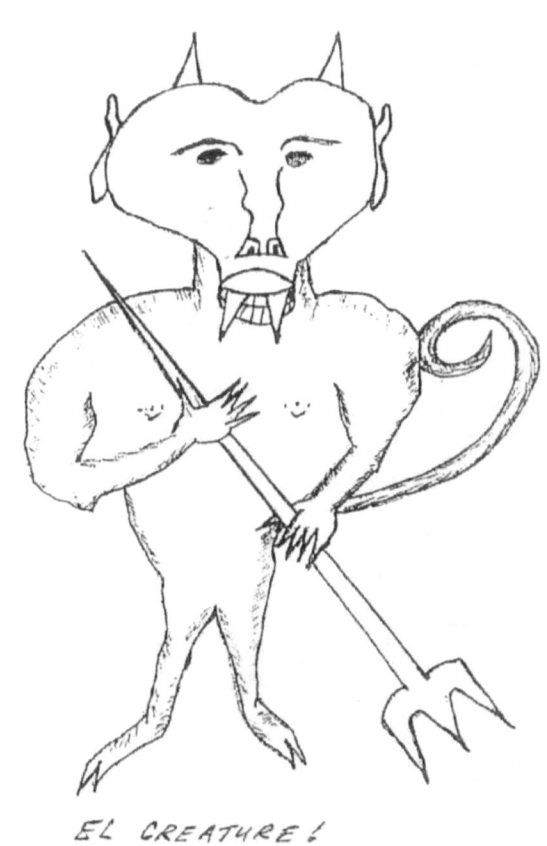

EL CREATURE!

La Liorna: Also known as the weeping lady, she comes out at night, dressed in white, with a skull face, weeping for her children who drowned in *El Rio Grande*. And, as folklore goes, it is said that she comes around the old pump house on the nearby levy in search of children she can capture. She, too, protects the treasure.

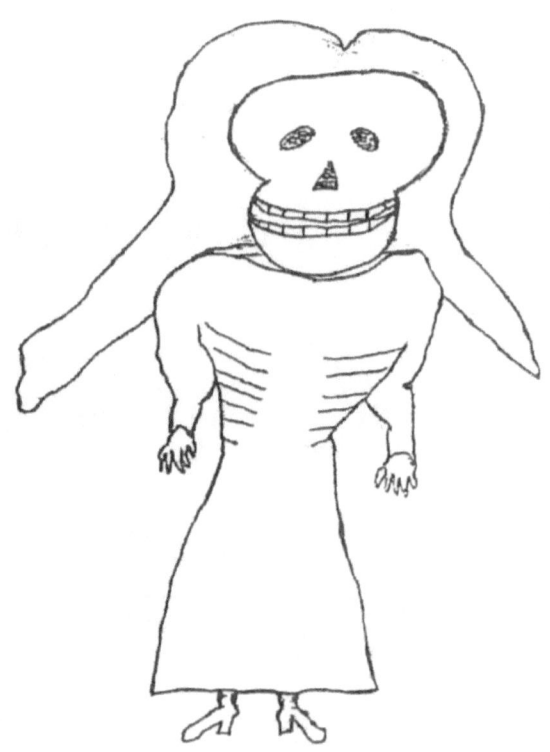

LA LLORONA 1

La Mujer Vestida de Blanco: She holds the keys to the old *camposanto* cemetery and also protects the treasure. She seeks living souls to take to the creature.

LA MUJER VESTIDA DE BLANCO!

El Hombre Sin Cabeza (the man without a head): As folklore goes, this innocent man was hanged in the old Hidalgo County Jail behind the Old Hidalgo County Courthouse after having been lynched for stealing cattle. He lost his head and now comes out at night, hunting for his head. He is also known as The Headless Man.

EL HOMBRE SIN CABEZA !

118

(Summer Breeze! Artist's sketch *Las Compuertas*)
La Lechuza: Also known as the owl or night bird
that makes whistling and shrieking sounds at

night. It is known to spray a liquid poison towards people, and to use its long nails like scissors to harm people. *La Luchuza* is one of the *Fantasmas* that also protects the treasure.

LA Lechuza

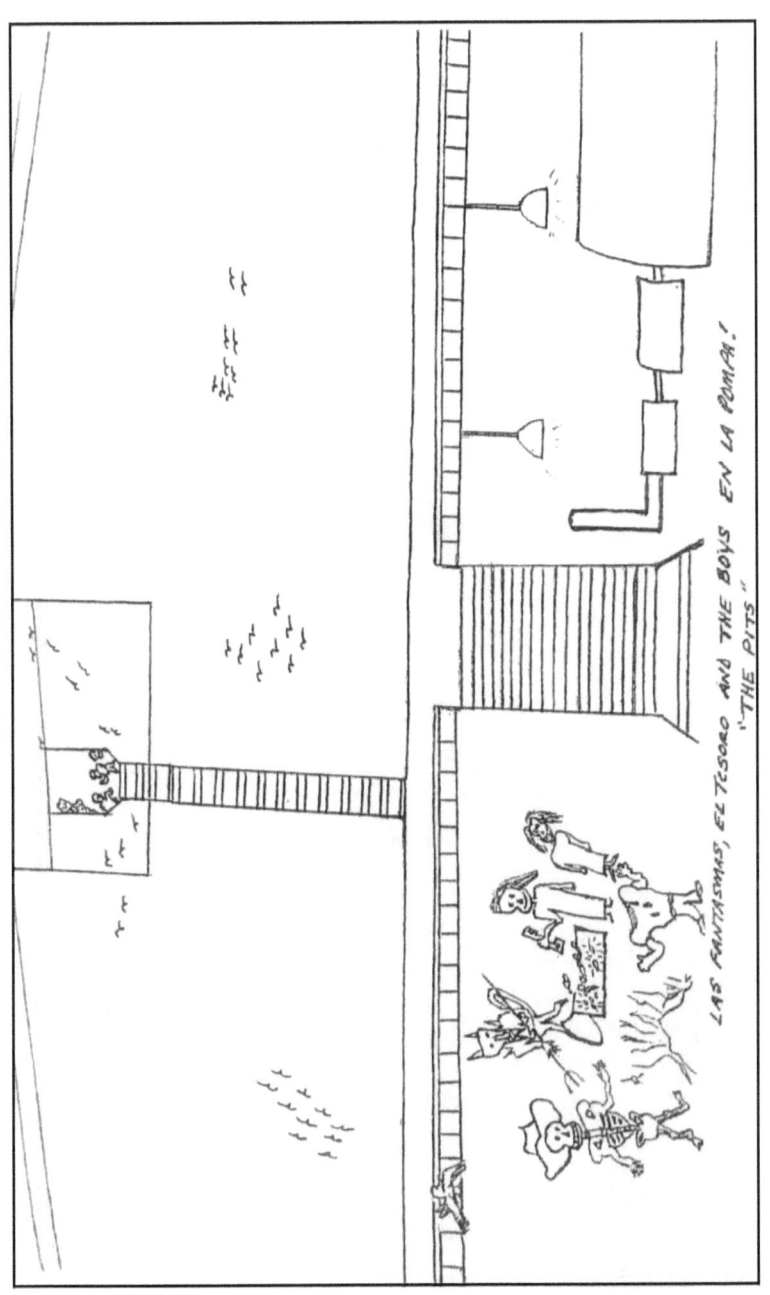

LAS FANTASMAS, EL TESORO AND THE BOYS EN LA ROMPA! "THE PITS"

121

Boys find and recover the Hidalgopirates
treasure, held by *Las Fantasmas.*

RICHIE EXORCISING LAS FANTASMAS FROM LUISITO!

Don Luis   Alfredo   La Muerta
by la pits en La Pompa

124

Special Edition II
"ONCE UPON A TIME AROUND OLD HIDALGO"

History of Old Hidalgo Pumphouse

[Old Hidalgo Aerial View]

Welcome to Old Hidalgo. Constructed in 1909, the pump house enshrined its surroundings, which were established circa 1886.

As seen by the view from the Hidalgo

County Court House built in 1886, (see photo above taken in 1916) and photo of courthouse before reconstruction, the Hidalgo Pump House was situated next to the Rio Grande River. The course of the river was altered by a major hurricane in 1933 diverting it to its present trajectory. This, therefore, made it a requirement to form a channel from the river to reach the pump house, so that thousands of gallons of water could be pumped into the canals that would distribute water for the nearby acres of crops. Additionally, the photo shows some historical spots that were very influential in the history and development of both the county and city of Hidalgo, which is important to mention. There used to be a levy cutting across a vacant area next to what is now known as 1st Street, Flora Street and Bridge Street, where Phillip Garcia's U.S. Custom Broker Warehouse business stands. The area was west from the two-story house also known

The original Hidalgo County courthouse and jail were constructed on the northern bank of the Rio Grande in 1886. Built of handmade Mexican brick, the courthouse originally had two stories and a cupola, but the second floor, the roof, and the cupola were destroyed by fire early in the 20th century. The courthouse later became a customs house. The courthouse and jail today house the offices of the Hidalgo County Historical Commission.

Gerardt, Karen and Rod Santa Ana II. Hidalgo County, Texas. Images of America Series. Chicago: Arcadia Publishing, C. 2000

128

as Humble Gas Station, which also served as a merchandise grocery store. Built in 1889, it was operated by Federico Rodriguez along with his wife, Lolita, descendants of Desiderio Rodriguez. During the primary years of Hidalgo, the little Humble Gas Station, along with selling gas and kerosene, also sold flour, beans, baking powder, lard, dry milk, various cheeses, salami, sausage, coffee, and other dry goods and produce. There were even a few shelves stacked with clothes and shoes to be sold or products that could be ordered by catalog.

Then, as the years passed, Federico Rodriguez and his wife Lolita Resendez Rodriguez gave birth to three sons and three daughters; one of those daughters was also named Lolita. She, in turn, married Benino Alonzo. At the time, Benino sold insurance and catalog goods. Then after marrying Lolita, Benino began to assist his in-laws with the small Humble Gas Station and grocery store, which remained in business for many more years after old Don Federico and Doña Lolita passed away.

At the same time, Benino and Lolita were blessed with a son, whom they named Mamiliano Alonzo. He was known to his friends as Mami. Then as Mami was going to the Hidalgo Elementary School (now the oldest school in the county) he and *Erasmo* "Mito" Rivera, Jr. became good friends. Incidentally, as the history of an area goes through word of mouth from generation to generation, in the early 1900's the vacant lot across the Humble Gas Station became populated with people coming from Mexico and Spain. Some of these settlers worked for the Hidalgo Pumphouse, which in turn allowed them to settle the land surrounding the pump house. One of the first settlers was Bartolo Rivera and his wife Irene Rocha who built a small mud and wooden frame house on the corner of Gardenia and 1st Street while he worked in the pump house. Irene gave birth to twelve kids, including several sons (Viviano, Gilberto, Luis, Paulino, Erasmo and Juan) who from time to time assisted their father Bartolo work around the pump house. Luis was the only one to dedicate his efforts and labor to the pump house, where he worked nearly sixty years. He would retire from the pump house and live with his wife Pabla (Pala) in the historical house located in the corner of 2nd and Gardenia (see photo, Rivera's house). They were blessed with many nephews and nieces.

[Spanish Language Newspaper Clipping.]

Rostro de Cristo appeared to Doña Pabla February 29, 1983

in Rivera's house, now Pabla's Café

[Doña Pabla and Antonia's altar to *Cristo*]

132

One day, while making corn *gorditas,* the image of Jesus Christ appeared on one of the *tortillas* to Pabla, which she showed to her sister-in-law Antonia Rivera. After receiving acknowledgment and confirmation from the Catholic Church of the authenticity of Christ's image on the edible item, Doña Pabla and Antonia built an alter for the image of *Cristo.*

*M*any people came from various parts of the world to ask for blessings and *milagros.* Many years later, kitty-corner to Luis, moved the late Johnny Franz and his family, Mayor John David Franz's father. The Anaya family used to live there before them in the early sixties.

At anv rate, the whole area around the pump house became populated by those employed by the Hidalgo Pump House or nearby establishments. West from the historical house on Gardenia lived Frank and Juanita Castillo. Next to them lived Memo Munguia "El boy" (of the Alfonso Munguia family), who was one of the first Hidalgo Police Officers. His sister, Consuelo, had a small party store where she sold soda waters, snacks and kerosene for the early use of stoves. Further west lived Paulino and Gabriela Rivera along with their family, who bought the land from Eduardo Vela, Sr. He was Hidalgo's mayor for many years, followed by his son Eduardo Vela, Jr. who became Hidalgo's mayor for many years, too. Doña Gabriela also had a little store where she sold candy at five cents each and *raspas* of different flavors.

Later on, as their kids grew, Paulino Rivera Jr. and his wife Petra bought a lot from Paulino's parents right next to where the levy used to stand. East from Paulino and Gabriela, Rogelio Rivera and his family obtained a piece of land, too. Nonetheless, south of them in one of the two small yellow houses in front of the pump house lived this man known as *El Zapatero*; then Luis Sweet, and then Jose Perales and family. Luis Rivera lived on the east side in a small yellow house before moving into the Gardenia house, where Rufus Wisdom and his family had lived first. He then moved to the rear of the pump house a few yards southeast to where the birding center now stands. While further west, directly behind the pump house, lived other pump house workers, like Mr. Bush and family. Then later Walter Wisdom, one of Rufus' son, who worked for the pump house and ended up working in the new Electrical Hidalgo Pumphouse still under the Hidalgo County Irrigation No. 2.

Getting back to the little Humble Gas Station and two-story building, this was also where Mami and Mito began to train and box together. Their goals and endeavors were to become Golden Glove champions and eventually turn professional someday. Mami loved to workout so much that one day he persuaded his parents, Lolita and Benino, to allow him to use the bottom part of the two-story building as a training gym for boxing and weightlifting. There, Mami and Mito trained daily after running down the levy next to the Rio Grande Bend, where the Hidalgo-Reynosa International Bridge was constructed.

[Rivera House – Built 1895]

They also trained with their teacher, Mr. Arcemendez, at the old elementary located on 324 E. Flora, which was built in 1898.

Moreover, directly south of the two-story building stands a small house where Beto Rodriguez lived. He was one of Don Federico Rodriguez' sons. He became a rich landowner around Reynosa, Tamalipas, Mexico. Beto's brother, Federico J., became a prominent businessman. Another sibling, Ramiro, assisted in getting the Hidalgo bridge built, becoming part owner with Mr. Bill Pate. At first there were only canoes that crossed folks from the Mexican side to the U.S. Years later in the early sixties, Jesse Daugherty and family set roots in the City of Hidalgo, where his daughter, Sylvia, has worked most of her life.

The following information has been shared by Erasmo Rivera, Jr. (Mito), who is originally from Hidalgo and was born in the early 1930's in the old Hidalgo County Courthouse. That old courthouse had become a boarding house after its facilities had been relocated further north from the Rio Grande River to what is now known as the city of Edinburg, Texas. There, in the old courthouse, Mito's parents Erasmo Rivera, Sr. and Petra Garcia, rented a boarding room and gave birth to Erasmito. They later moved to a small, two-room wooden house located southwest and in front of the Humble Gas Station.

Through the years a steady stream of settlers from Spain and Mexico continued to come into the area. Some of the original settlers around Hidalgo were the Ayala, Alonzo Vasquez, Hernandez, Rodriguez. Rocha, Rivera, Garcia, Munguia, Valenzuela, Samano, Vela, Tagle, Perez, Gonzales, Davila, Castillo, Cortinas, Fuentes, Zepedas, Montemayor, Garza, Guerrero, Guerra, Duke, Paz, Baker, Pate, Blanco, Vargas, Diaz, Arismendez, Alcalda, Acevedo, Valdez, Villareal, Villagomez, Uribe, Ureste, Sanchez, Serano, Reyes, Valdivia, Wisdom, and Franz families. (Please forgive any unintentional omissions of other family names). Members of many of the above stated families are still living and working for, and in, the City of Hidalgo.

Such landowners like Mr. Bill Pate, Fugencio "Kencho" Gonzalez, Eduardo Vela, Sr., and others depended fully on the Hidalgo Pump House and *el* Rio Grande River for their crops to prosper on a yearly basis. All these landowners and their families were also very influential in the growth of the city and the county of Hidalgo. There used to be cattle below the levy that held the canals taking the pump water to irrigate the crops close to where many colorful peacocks ran freely around the Tejano Lake. Eventually, the canals were re-routed and filled with dirt, as a new electric pump was constructed around the bend of *El Rio Grande* making way for new routes and reservoirs.

Furthermore, Don Bartolo, who raised a family of twelve, was fortunate to get a job constructing the Hidalgo Pump House, where he worked with Anglo supervisors such as Van Dresser, Cramer and others. Don Bartolo trained his son, Luis Rivera, on how to keep the furnaces burning to create enough steam for the huge steam engines, which propelled the river stream into the canals to irrigate the crops on the United States side in the county of Hidalgo. Thus, this effort made the area very fertile for various crops such as sugar cane, tomatoes, carrots, cabbage, cauliflower, chili peppers, onions, cotton, cantaloupe, watermelons, grapefruit, and mangos among others. Don Luis also built his small, two-room house across the street from Humble Gas Station (see photo Humble Gas Station) before moving closer to the pump house area. Year later his *hijo de crianza,* Luis Rivera, Jr. and his wife, Maria, would move into the two-room house. Consequently, the whole area that was empty in front of the Humble Gas Station and Grocery Store quickly became populated by Hidalgo's subsequent settlers like the Rocha (see photo in front), Rivera, Garcia, Samano, and Franz families.

Of the Franz family, Alberto Franz married Anita Rocha, who was Don Ausencio and Aurelia Rocha's daughter. They had several kids who first attended the Hidalgo Elementary School before moving to Palm Springs, California. At the time, California had become an area of opportunity for many poor folks from South Texas. Then in the corner of 1st and Flora streets used to live Ausencio "Chencho" Rocha, Jr. and his family, who ultimately also moved to California. When Don Ausencio, Sr. passed away, Aurelia stayed behind to raise their daughters and the rest of her grandsons and granddaughters, some being from the Chavelo Vargas family. Furthermore, Don Ausencio, Sr. was Irene Rocha's brother. She had married Bartolo Rivera, who also worked at the Hidalgo Pumphouse.

North from the Rivera's lived Don Alberto Samano, Sr. and his wife, Carolina, who used to love to keep a beautiful garden. And across from them lived Doña San Juanita Alcalda and her sons, Pancho and Beto Alcalda, where Pancho "*El Poco Poco*" used to have a small storage room in front of the old courthouse for his candy boxes. The candy bars used to cost five cents a bar in the fifties. At any rate, all this area has been reconstructed by the Texas State Bank, which later became BBVA Compass Bank. But before the bank was constructed in the late sixties the levy was still blocking the progress and expansion of the City of Hidalgo, at least until a committee spearheaded by Pedro *"La Pirucha"* Garcia, an Hidalgo Alderman, and then

Mayor Enedina Garza, convinced the Hidalgo County
Commissioners and Corps of Engineers that the Levy was
no longer necessary to protect the city from flooding. This
was because there was already a levy to the south, next to
the Rio Grande *Resaca* and around the *rio* and International
Bridge. That levy has been paved around the Hidalgo
Pumphouse for bike trails and runs east to west along
the river going under the international bridge.
Now Border Patrol Homeland Security go up and
down the levies.

Therefore, the levy was bulldozed after
Pirucha bought the piece of land from Aurelia
Rocha and her family, naming it the Pirucha
Subdivision. This transformation not only
allowed Pirucha to build a bigger store and
several warehouses, but it also allowed the city
to construct Bridge Street along with several
businesses and Banks; thus, allowing it to
expand. Now there was more to the city than just
gas stations on the opposite corners south and
north of what used to be South 23rd Street, now
known as Esperanza and Bridge Street, like the
Sinclair, Shamrock and the Texaco gas station

(which was operated by Alberto Samano, Jr. and Lucila, along with their gas attendant Chito). Then there was the Crowflight behind where the Flint National Bank now stands; and a produce store on the southeast corner of Esperanza and Bridge Street, where The Texas State Bank was built (now Compass Bank) near the old Hidalgo Courthouse and County Jail.

Another little grocery store in Hidalgo that merits mentioning, and which was used by the Rio Grande Valley Bus Station system as a bus stop for its customers going towards McAllen, was the Cipriano Samano Grocery Store located at the corner of Dalia and Bridge Street. In fact, it was also used as a high school bus stop for students from Hidalgo going to McAllen High School (as there was no high school in Hidalgo in the early 1960's). South of Dalia street was Hidalgo's old post office. Now returning to the area around the two-story home, as the story goes, Ramiro Rodriguez married Melba, who was Mr. Baker's sister. Mr. Baker was Hidalgo's school principal and school board member for many years. He even became one of Hidalgo's mayors; while his wife, Mrs. Baker, was a tough first grade teacher in the Hidalgo Elementary School (which at first was located at 324 Flora Street as mentioned earlier but, eventually moving into the new building across the street). Additionally, while Ramiro and Melba were married, they adopted a child whom they named Lindsey Rodriguez. After receiving his higher education, Lindsey became a prominent Texas Politician in the 1960's.

Toward the end of that decade, Lolita built a new brick house east of the two-story home, where after her death, the house mysteriously burned down. However, before the whole area where this house and the Hidalgo Municipal Court was developed, there were some corrals with cattle and longhorns kept by Don Refugio "Don Cuco" Valenzuela and his sons. Don Cuco owned a lot of cattle, becoming one of Hidalgo's first milkmen by sending his sons, Chato and Richie, to deliver milk and cream to various families around Hidalgo and the surrounding areas.

On the opposite side of Flora street lived Alberto Samano, Jr. and his wife, Lucila, with their family. Their son became Mayor pro-tem Alvin Samano. Right behind Lucila's house is a tiny little house where Doña Antonia Rivera lived for many years, making corn tortillas to sell, and babysitting far Lucila from time to time. This tiny house was also a few steps away from the old 1886 Hidalgo Post Office and a few yards opposite the Humble Gas Station (Photo on next page).

History takes its toll, and what had been built throughout the years in the corner of 1st, Gardenia and Flora streets has taken another transformation. All the old houses that had been built and apartments Pirucha had rented out have now been demolished. As the Hidalgo Pumphouse has become a tourist's attraction as a Historical Museum and Birding center.

[Humble Gas Station under construction]

The State of Texas, The Historical Commission, the Hidalgo City Council, the Hidalgo Chamber of Commerce (spearheaded by city manager Mr. Joe Vera), the pump house staff and present director—along with Viola Aresmendez, past Directors Chuck Snyder, Kay Wolf, Hidalgo city employees, and other volunteers—have all decided to make further additions to the birding center and it's nature trails; thus, transforming the landscape around the Hidalgo Pumphouse. This not only preserves the history of the City of Hidalgo, but it highlights the beauty of this place through its nature trails and through the contributions of its formidable Historical Museum, and now the District of Hidalgo, Tx.

The sounds of the running water can still be heard in the distance coming through the *compuertas* of *el canal,* the all-time favorite swimming and fishing spot for many local youth and area elders like Simone Vargas, as well as for those living around the Tejano lake and *el capote*, where past Mayor Thomas Perez, Jr. and immediate family used to live near *los canales cuates*. Undoubtedly, this iconic Texas landmark represents much more than a simple mechanism for the delivery of water for crops and grazing cattle. It symbolizes a people and their city, as well as a moment in the story of America

HIDALGO, EL DORADO by Lucio G. Rivera

I am Hidalgo, El Dorado
Who shines enlightening the hearts
and minds of those who seek the light.
The Wisdom and knowledge of why you see what is in
front of you.
Only those who seek love, wisdom, knowledge and
understanding come to me.

I am Hidalgo, El Dorado

Who will never change.

I am love and respect for those who yearn for sympathy,
courage and strength
To take another step forward in their struggles

To survive against the harsh storms of life.

Like a lashing whip, I will get things right from the heart
For those who believe in me.

I am Hidalgo, El Dorado

Who will never change his name

For I am blessed to open the gates where I will shine
brighter than a star at night:
Gold, silver, pearls, and diamonds,

I have class and style and will lead you into the beauty of
life.

I will share with you the wonderful things of life and nature.

I am Hidalgo. El Dorado

Who will not let you down.

I will steer the way through good and bad times;

Take you down and up the longest Rio Grande nature has formed

With heavenly reasons to share life with us.

There will never be valleys wide enough or mountain banks tall enough
To keep me from being reached and adored.

I am Hidalgo, El Dorado forever and ever ....

Pictures were provided courtesy of
PCT Photo Archives

Pic#1
Armando Gonzalez, Guadalupe Nuñez, Giahiza Zapata, &
Cecilio Muñoz flank Sebastian Correa, back in 2011.
Pg 56

Pic#2
Alejandro Arango, Jose Luis Hinojosa & Rolando Garcia III
onstage; J.P. Peña, Bryan McIntire, & Javier Robles offstage.
Pg 57

Pic#3
Jaden Allen, Liliana Martinez, Gianna Eason, Emily May and
Kaylah Killian.
Pg 58

Pic#4
Evita Tijerina as El Hombre Sin Cabeza, Giahiza Zapata as
La Lechuza, Cecilio Muñoz at La Muerte & Guadalupe
Nuñez as La llorona.
Pg 59

Pic#5
Jose Luis Hinojosa played Luis Rivera and Rolando Garcia
III played Rufus Wisdom.
Pg 60

Pic#6
Javier Robles as Luisito and Armando Gonzalez as El Pirata.
Pg 61

Pic#7
Isabel Muñoz plays the talkative Tia Toñita.
Pg 62

Pic#8
Wally Gonzalez, aka, "The Short-Legged Texan", sitting with Co-author Pedro Garcia, wrote a fun song for the play called *La Pompa de Hidalgo*.
Pg 63

Pic#9
The old Pump House now a museum and world birding center in Hidalgo, TX
Pg 64

Pic#10
Jose Luis Hinojosa as Luis Rivera, Pamela Dougherty as Paula Rivera and Evita Tijerina as El Hombre sin Cabeza performing a hilarious scene.
Pg 65

Pic#11
Author Lucio G. Rivera & his wife Alma take a stroll at a Frida Kahlo Fest in Edinburg, TX.
Pg 66

Pic#12
The original poster for the premier in 2011.
Pg 67

Author Bios

Lucio G. Rivera is a writer with several novels that are awaiting publishing including:

The Streets of Detroit and The Underground Drug Web. His plays include Purple Shaded Heart and In and Out Dayroom and is currently working on "Adventures Around the Hidalgo Pumphouse."

Rivera grew up in Hidalgo, TX and Detroit Michigan, where he graduated from Wayne State University. He was a member of the Chicano-Boricua Studies program of Monteith College. He currently resides in Hidalgo, TX and is a certified Electrician employed by Phillip Garcia, U.S. Custom Brokers. He continues to write on his spare time, most recently about Hidalgo, TX history.

Pedro Garcia has been an active member of the Screen Actors Guild since 1994.

He has directed and acted in over 100 plays since 1987. He's appeared on several films and TV shows including, Mad Love, Fast & Furious Five, Breaking Bad & Halt & Catch Fire.

Currently he resides in Pharr, TX and is the Artistic Director for the Pharr Community Theater Co. in Pharr, TX. He also works as a freelance talent finder and casting assistant in the RGV. He is represented by Legacy Talent Agency out of Austin, TX.

He can be reached at: teatronuestra@hotmail.com
(See his full resume at www.nowcasting.com/pedrogarcia)

About Legado Publishing

El Legado de la Frontera

Legado Publishing es una editorial del Valle del Rio Grande en el sur de Tejas. Nuestra meta es elevar el perfil de escritoras y escritores de la región, inclusive del lado mexicano de la frontera. Buscamos autoras y autores emprendedores y motivados a establecer su marca en el mundo literario y dejar una huella que sirva a otros a seguir. Es decir, construir un legado artístico que utilice distintas formas para desenvolver el carácter creativo de la gente de la frontera de Estados Unidos y México.

Para más información visite la página web:
legadopublishing.info

Correo electrónico:
                    legadopublishing@gmail.com